The Sword From The Sky

A Book of
The Abyss Walker World

by

Patrick S. Tomlinson

Cover art by Kendall R. Hart.

Interior layout and design by Kendall R. Hart.

Editing services provided by William Tracy and Edward Gehlert.

Foreword written by Shane Moore.

Beta reading performed by Sandra Wagner.

A New Babel Books Release

381 High Point Drive

Holiday Shores, IL 62025

Genre: Fantasy / Series

ISBN: 978-1-63196-025-3

First Printing.

Printed in the United States of America.

wrung the sweat from it. Then he reached in with the tongs to begin again.

Just as the clanging of the hammer was about to resume, the smith saw movement outside his window. There were only a handful of reasons people would be lurking about at this time of night, few of which were terribly encouraging. Annoyed, the smith threw the billet back into the forge. He pulled the beeswax from his ears and walked quietly through the door into the display room of his shop.

Still holding the heavy shaping hammer, he peeked through a window. A shadowy figure clung close to the wall. The smith slipped out the front door and around into the garbage-strewn alley. With stealth, surprising for such a large frame, he crept up on the figure from behind. His free hand reached out and grabbed the intruder's tunic.

Panicked, the figure tried to bolt but the smith's grip was as strong as the iron he had spent a lifetime working.

"Only a drunkard, a thief, or an idiot would be prying the shadows at this late hour. Tell me, which are you?"

The intruder twisted his head around to get a look at the man anchoring him. "None, good sir, I assure you!"

"Explain yourself." The smith raised his hammer in warning, but his captive threw up his hands.

"I wish to barter!"

An idiot, then. The smith rolled his eyes. "Bartering comes with the sun. Why did you not wait 'till morning'?"

"I've just arrived in the city, and saw light in your window. I heard you working still, and was about to go and fetch my sack to show you my wares."

The smith smirked. "Well then you won't mind if we walk to your bag, together." He nearly lifted the squirrelly man from his feet and started walking down the alley.

"Where is it?"

"It's just ahead, to the left." Indeed, there was a large, fraying, burlap sack propped up against the back of the smith's shop.

Prologue

The hammer fell through the sweltering air of the smith's workshop.

Clang!

The glowing-hot piece of iron deformed under the blow of the hammer, one strike closer to becoming a woodsman's ax.

Clang!

The sound was earsplitting; so much so, that the smith had taken to plugging his ears with beeswax in recent years, to protect what remained of his hearing.

Clang!

The orange glow faded to blood red, then disappeared entirely. Grabbing the billet with tongs, the smith walked over to his forge and set the metal inside. He was working late into the night and his new apprentice had already gone off to sleep. But he had remaining work in the form of the new flywheel he'd cobbled together for the bellows.

The smith smiled to himself as he spun the great stone wheel a little faster. It was hard to start, but once it was in motion, the wheel was equally hard to stop. A swing arm connected to the bellows and the forge's fire burned white hot. The wheel had transformed the forge into a one-man job.

After less than a minute in the inferno, the billet was back to a working color. The smith removed his head cloth and

"There will come a day when the heavens turn their back on us as the shadows rise up to claim our lands. Only the humbled one can be our salvation when he discovers who walks for death. Yet, even then, if his love is lost, the darkness will be lasting."

~ Hiramem's Prophecy

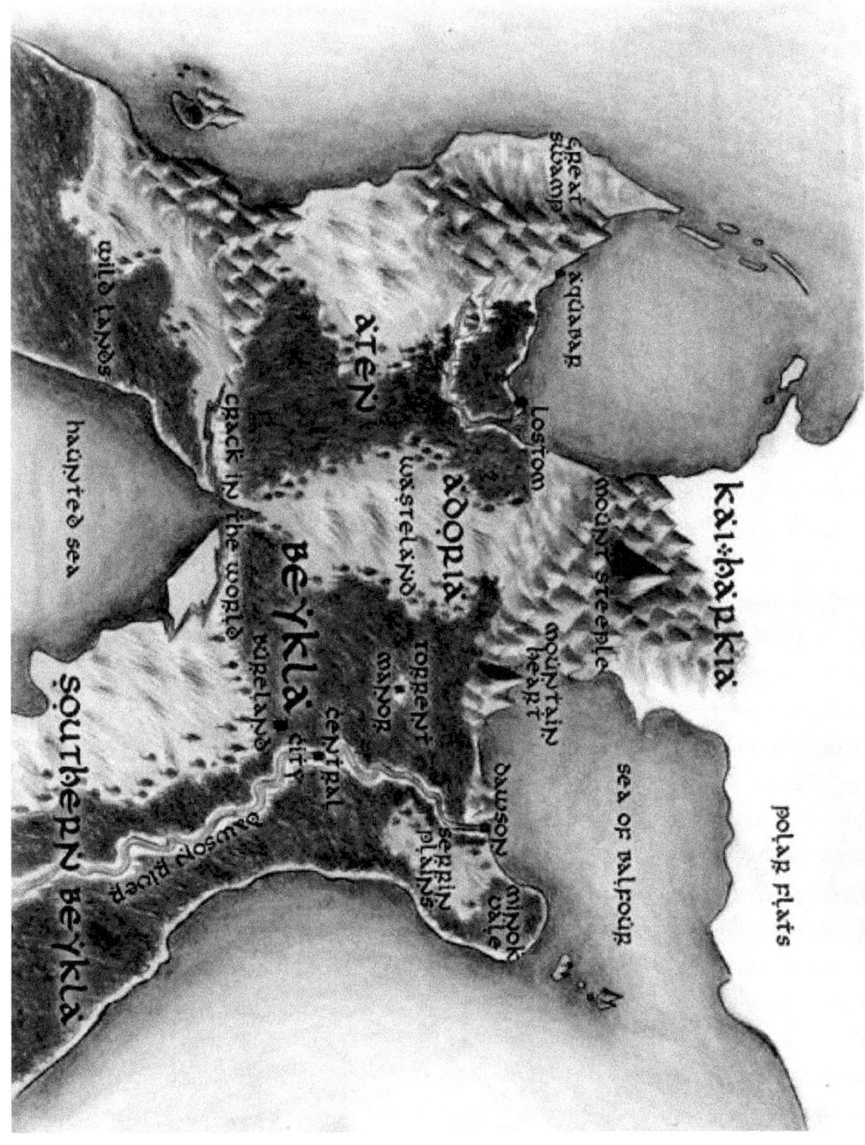

Foreword

To the Abyss Walker fans. Despite the bankruptcy of a publisher, the collapse of a major chain, and the evolving industry--you made this happen!

The smith relaxed his grip. The hammer hung menacingly in the air between them. "Open it. Slowly."

The trader held out his hands and walked gingerly to the sack. The smith noticed that his gangly guest had a pronounced limp in his left leg. The trader untied the drawstrings and held open the flap. By the moonlight, the smith could just make out rusted bits of plate armor, fragments of shields, arrowheads, and broken blades of all sizes and shapes.

Great, a vulture, the smith thought bitterly. It was inevitable. With all the battles that had ravaged his home of Central City lately, the scavengers of battlefields would not be far behind. The thought of the war dead having their corpses picked clean by these morbid creatures was enough to turn his stomach.

Still, battle-steel was among the finest made. The bagful of metal would work into fine tools and save him enormous effort. The smith could turn a handsome profit, if he could get it at the right price. Practicality allowed him to swallow his misgivings. He nodded to the trader. "We can talk. Bring it inside."

"Could you lend me a hand? It is quite heavy, and my leg is somewhat diminished."

The smith laughed spitefully and pointed at the injury. "One of your customers not quite dead while you accepted his donation?"

The vulture averted his eyes. "Something like that."

The smith grabbed hold of one side of the sack and heaved. It was indeed heavy, even for his stout arms. He wondered how such a slight man had gotten it this far in the first place, but dismissed the thought.

Once inside the front room of his shop, the smith slashed open the side of the bag with a small dagger kept hidden in his smock. The contents clanged out onto the floor. Most of it was battered and rusted. The sword and dagger blades were nicked and dull from heavy use, and what few intact pieces of armor remained were dinged and pitted from intense combat. They could not be reused as weapons.

The smith inspected the pile closely. Most of the arrowheads were curled or blunted from striking shields or breastplates, but the tips could be reshaped well enough for the hunt. Game animals weren't generally known for donning metal armor. There were also quite a few pieces of broken orcish weapons. Orc craftsmen were generations behind the civilized races, and their metal showed it. It was brittle, couldn't hold an edge for long, and rusted easily. It was nearly useless.

The smith sighed. "I'll have no need for the pig iron. That leaves with you."

"You would know better than I," said the vulture, "However, you have torn my sack, and there are too many pieces to carry by hand."

"Then I will deduct the cost of disposing of it from the final price." The smith looked down at the vulture, expecting him to rise to the bait. He wanted to haggle from a position of strength, and to keep his opponent off balance. But the vulture simply nodded.

"That's fine. I was thinking twenty gold for the set, so let's call it nineteen."

"Five, or you leave with the whole pile, not just the pig iron."

"Fine. Five it is."

Now it was the smith caught off balance. Five gold was an absurd price for so much battle-steel, even in a buyer's market. He'd picked it just to low-ball the vulture, hoping to draw him towards the middle, but he'd relented without so much as a huff of protest. Something about the whole situation smelled like the fish-market on a summer afternoon.

The smith casually spun the dagger between his fingers. "You wouldn't be using this little negotiation to case my shop, by any chance?"

The vulture's eyes darted back and forth between the

dagger and the pile of scrap on the floor. "No, not at all. I'm just eager to get back on the road. You'll probably never see me again."

Still, the smith's eyes narrowed to slits. "You won't mind waiting outside then, while I get your payment."

"Not at all. Just call when you're ready." He jaunted through the door into the darkened streets. The state of affairs raised the hairs on the back of the smith's neck. But so long as the vulture didn't see where the shop's gold was kept, he couldn't see any real trouble coming of it.

He returned to the back room and, using the tongs, pulled a thick iron safe out from a space sunk into the floor just beneath the forge. With a gloved hand, he opened the lid and gingerly picked out five gold coins, their portraits softened by the heat of the fire above. He dipped them into the slack tank, sending a puff of steam towards the ceiling. After a minute, they were cool enough to handle.

The smith returned to the storefront and called for the vulture.

"You have it, then?" he asked greedily.

The smith simply held up his arm and dropped the five yellow coins into the vulture's waiting palm. His lips curled into a sneer. "Pleasure doing business with you."

Without another word, the scavenger pocketed the coins and limped off into the night. His footsteps shrank into the distance until there was nothing but the breeze whistling through the open door. Good to his word, the smith would never see him again.

Tired, but relieved the unsettling encounter was over, the smith turned back to the pile on his floor and started sorting it into two stacks; one for usable metal, the other for scraps and pig iron.

The rusty, pitted blades would not return to combat duty, but they could be fashioned into durable tools. Two daggers could be joined into shears with little effort. Broken swords bent nicely into scythes and sickles for harvesting grain.

His thoughts skidded to a stop as something lustrous near the bottom caught his eye. It was untarnished, free of rust and grime. Thinking he'd found a pearl among pebbles, the smith hurriedly dug through the pile to reach it. What he found was a sword blade, cracked, through where the tang met the pommel. The edge was still keen and unblemished.

It had been a magnificent sword, once. *A shame it can not be restored,* thought the smith. But there were other possibilities for it. It felt as though it would keep an edge well. The grain-lands to the southeast had soil of packed red clay. Fertile, but notoriously difficult to till. The farmers there paid generously for ploughshares that would last more than a single season. The remaining blade was just long enough for such an item. The smith could make his entire investment back on this one piece, perhaps more.

Excitedly, he stood and turned towards the forge with renewed energy, eager to resume work. Yet as he walked through the doorway, his elbow struck the frame, jolting the blade just enough to deeply cut his palm. He felt the sting and the sword clanged on the floor. So sharp and clean was the cut that several moments passed before the blood-ways realized they had been severed. Then, crimson erupted into the smith's cupped palm. He cursed, then wrapped his hand with a strip of cloth and returned to the stifling heat of the forge.

The drumbeat of the hammer began again.

Clang!

Clang!

Clang!

The rays of the midday sun rained down onto Ansel Deepspade's neck and shoulders like molten lead. It was still early in the season, but this year was proving to be an unusually hot and parched one. But, as his father delighted in reminding him, they couldn't wait around for the wizards to invent self-tilling soil. Probably wouldn't like the cost if they ever did, for that matter.

The heat was also failing to inspire any urgency from Stump, the Deepspade family's plow mule. He had stopped mid-furrow to snack on a dandelion. Stump was so named because when they had first bought him four seasons ago to help clear tree roots from a new field, it wasn't immediately apparent whose side he was on. Stump took the long view in life; if he waited long enough, someone would have to feed him.

"Yaa, Stump. Yaa, mule." Ansel snapped on the reins with gusto, but Stump's head simply swung back and regarded him with a look that conveyed that work would resume when he had finished his salad, and not a moment before. This was a fairly complicated message for a mule to pass along, but he managed it.

"Fine, you daft creature, have it your way." Ansel's hand reached into a flap of his tunic and reappeared with a succulent yellow pear. Now, Ansel had Stump's undivided attention. Or at least the fruit did. Ansel's arm reared back and heaved the pear into a long arch through the sky.

Stump took off after it, like a bolt from a crossbow. Ansel struggled just to keep up, not to mention keeping the plow tilling straight and at the proper depth.

"Whoa, Stump! Whoa!" But the mule was moving with a purpose now, and paid Ansel the same measure of attention as before. They ran across the field, churning over a furrow of the devilish red clay as they went. Stump's galloping feet kicked up a cloud of brick-colored dust directly into Ansel's face. Maybe the pear hadn't been the best idea after all.

A sharp crack like thunder rang from the ground. The plow heaved up out of the soil and fell to its side, spilling Ansel onto the dirt. Undeterred, or just unconcerned, Stump dragged it right on, to the end of the row, and started a furious search for the missing pear.

Huffing with effort, and covered in sweat and rusty dirt, Ansel finally caught up to the errant equine. He stooped over to inspect any damage to the plow. The frame and coulter were fine, as was the mouldboard that turned the dirt. But, much to his horror, the ploughshare had been shattered.

Without even going back to look, Ansel knew the crack he'd heard had been the share striking a rock. This was made doubly bad, due to the fact picking the field clean of rocks had been one of Ansel's jobs last season. His father would not be amused.

His pear expedition proving fruitless, Stump looked back at the plow with feigned interest. After sizing up the scene and carefully weighing the various factors, Stump decided that work had come to an end for the day. Preferring shade to the relentless sun, he ambled towards his shed, dragging the injured plow behind him without consulting Ansel, or even waiting for his harness to be removed; one of the two-legs would come along and do so eventually anyway and his shed had the benefit of a water basin.

Feeling defeated, Ansel watched Stump go, without lifting a finger to stop him. He was more concerned about his immediate future, and his survival prospects therein.

Dragging heavy feet, he marched towards the stone walls and thatch roof of the family farmstead. Outside in the yard stood Ansel's little sister, Elanir, her faded blue dress streaked with red dirt at the knees. She cradled a fluffy yellow chick in her hand and giggled as he approached.

"It keeps chirping at me," she observed as Ansel approached.

"It's probably mad you haven't fed it yet."

This made her laugh more. "Are you an angry little chicken?"

The chick made it known that, while not quite angry, it was at least perturbed.

"Put it down and feed the chickens, Itty."

Elanir dropped the chick and put on her best pouting face. "Don't call me Itty!"

"Don't be so little, then." Ansel stepped through the open door into the dining area. His father, Yorick, looked up from the work in his lap and nodded to his youngest son.

"I heard Stump coming back to the shed. Have you finished plowing already?"

"Not exactly, Sir."

Yorick paused, then gently placed the woodworking chisel and hammer onto the table. He wasn't a shouter, and he'd only raised a lash to the kids once each. He didn't need such crude tools. Yorick's gaze of disapproval could dig wells.

"And, why not?" he asked quietly.

Ansel inspected the floorboards by his feet. "Because the ploughshare's busted." Yorick's eyes asked the next question.

"I hit a rock in the field."

"A rock." Yorick nodded deliberately. "Is the share blunted, can it be sharpened?"

Ansel shook his head. "No, Sir. It's broke clean through in two places."

"A big rock, then. Hard for a picker to miss."

Ansel shrank. "Yes, Sir." He could see the gaze starting to

form and tried to run ahead of it. "I can go into the village and get a new one and still be back by the evening."

Yorick put a finger to his lips while considering this. "No," he said finally, "No, the smith in the village has always made brittle iron. If I had a better rock picker, that might not be a problem. But in this case… You will go to Central City and find the shop where your brother, Tiklan, apprentices. There you will buy a new ploughshare, the best available. But you are not to spend more than five gold on it. Do you understand?"

"Yes, Sir," Ansel said hesitantly, "But it's a four day walk there and back. Won't we fall behind for the planting?"

"Who said walk? Ride Stump. You can catch a barge at the Dawson River."

"But Stump never listens to me."

"Really?" Yorick arched a bushy eyebrow. "How peculiar. Stump listens to me."

Ansel frowned. Everything listened to Yorick. The weather was the only holdout, and he wasn't sure how much longer it could last.

"I will have a talk with Stump, then you will leave right after lunch, yes?"

"Yes, Father."

In truth, Ansel didn't fight his father's instruction too hard. He'd never been all the way to Central City by himself before. Only a few years ago, the prospect of being alone in such an enormous place would have terrified him.

Now, however, the chance to explore the big city brought curiosity and anticipation. He'd talked to some of the other farmers and seasonal hands who were more traveled than he was. He heard stories of the wild nights in pubs, where the beer flowed like a cresting river and men sang fighting songs until the sun returned. He also heard mention some of the more… lurid enticements cities had on offer. It was said a gold coin could buy an hour of your wildest fantasy in the harem houses of Central City. Ansel was old enough to know about *those* kinds of fantasy, even if he was still a little fuzzy on the specifics.

The family assembled for the noon meal. There were just the three of them now: Ansel, Yorick, and little Elanir. His two older brothers had moved on to learn a trade. There would be no more children either; his mother had passed away giving birth to Elanir. Some men in the village said that the Gods had abandoned man after some big battle. But for Yorick, the Gods died that night. He hadn't offered a prayer in years.

They ate simply, but heartily. Potatoes, carrots, scrambled eggs, year-old sharp cheese, and fresh milk to wash it all down.

"Is everyone full?" Yorick asked.

Elanir nodded her head vigorously, while Ansel merely shrugged.

"Good. Elanir, would you go and give Stump his oats, please?"

"Sure, Daddy." She hopped down from her chair and skipped out towards the shed. She was nothing if not eager to help, a rarity among little girls. Ansel wondered how long it would last.

Once she was gone, his father stood up from the table, the floorboards creaking under the weight of him. He walked over to the old oak cabinet, pulled out a small leather coin pouch, double-checked the contents, and tossed it to Ansel.

"That is your budget for the trip. Do not splurge. When you get close to the city, find a quiet place in the woods to tie off Stump so you don't have to pay for a stable. If you get lost in the city, find a guardsman and ask for help."

Yorick's voice dropped to a whisper as he leaned forward. "Also, you may see... things... in the city. Things you may not entirely understand. Ignore them. Don't go looking for trouble. Be polite and respectful to everyone you meet, but do not buy anything except the ploughshare. Do not move about after dark. Do not follow anyone, or offer to help. I know it sounds cruel, but trust me it's for your own safety. Do you understand, Ansel?"

"Yes, Sir. Absolutely."

"Good. Now, when you ignore my advice and screw up hopelessly, go find Tiklan. He will protect you."

Ansel couldn't help but grimace at the thought. Of everyone he knew, his middle brother Tiklan was possibly his least favorite. They had fought incessantly from the day he could walk until the day last year that Tiklan left for his apprenticeship in the city. Things had become much more peaceful in his absence.

His father handed him a trail pack. Inside was a healthy portion of smoked jerky, dried bread and berries, and a flint for starting fires.

Yorick cleared his throat. "Stump will be done with his oats by now. It's time to leave." His father came around the table and embraced him, his arms clamping around Ansel in a way he'd not felt in years. For a moment, he felt like a tiny boy again, safe and secure inside his father's infinite strength. All too soon, Yorick let go, and the moment was over.

"Be safe."

"I will." Ansel left for the shed at a leisurely pace, trying to hide his excitement. The *tap-tap-tap* of the hammer and chisel resumed behind him. Stump stood patiently in the shed, awaiting either Ansel or his next helping of oats. Ansel grabbed the bridle off a peg on the wall and slipped it over Stump's long face. Then he cinched a simple riding pad onto the mule's back.

"You're not going to give me any trouble on this trip, are you?"

Stump stared forward vacantly.

"Well, there's a fresh pear in it for you when we return, if you behave." A hairy ear stood up in response. "Ah, so you can hear me after all."

The ear fell back down, trying to pretend nothing had

happened. Ansel just shook his head and hopped onto the mule's back. He gave Stump's flank a little kick. "Yaa, mule."

With that, they were on the road to Central City and the adventure that would bring. The sun had started to climb down from its peak for the day, but the temperature was still climbing. Stump swatted away flies with his tail, while Ansel wiped beads of sweat from his forehead.

They had barely made it to the edge of the family's fields when something rustled in the trees behind him. Ansel's head snapped around to get a look at the source of the sound. He thought he caught a flash of light blue fluttering behind the trunk of an oak.

Ansel sighed in annoyance. "Come out here, Itty."

His sister stepped out from the tree and stamped her foot. "Don't call me Itty."

"Go home, Elanir."

She crossed her arms defiantly. "Daddy told me to come with you."

Ansel's eyes rolled clear to the back of his head. "Sure he did, Itty. Go home right now and I won't tell Father about your fibbing'."

"I'm not fibbin'!"

"Really? Okay, let's walk back together and ask him."

Elanir huffed and stamped her feet again. "It's not fair, I'm a big girl. I can do everything you do."

"Not this, Itty. The city is no place for a kid."

"You're still a kid!" she squealed.

"Father doesn't seem to think so." A small voice in the back of Ansel's mind hoped his father was right, but he wasn't going to let it show. "Go home. I'll see you in a couple days. I'll bring you a present."

This had the distracting effect he was hoping for. "Really, what kind of present?"

"I don't know yet. You'll just have to be patient."

"I want some of those shoes with the big heels, made out of emeralds."

"What's a farm girl going to do with emerald shoes?"

Elanir stared at him in mock confusion, as though the answer was self-evident. "Go to fancy dances, of course."

Ansel rubbed the bridge of his nose. "I don't think I've got enough money for that. I have to leave now Itty, or I'll miss the barge. Go home and help Father until I get back."

Elanir departed, still in a state, but somewhat placated by the prospect of shoes exceeding the total value of the entire family estate. The road beckoned, and Ansel spurred his ignoble steed onward.

The air in the archive felt ancient; mold spores and the smell of old parchment filled it until there was almost none left to breathe. A forest of bookcases, each as tall as two men, stood in perfect rows surrounding a central atrium. In front of one such case, a semi-circle of books, scrolls, and clay tablets radiated out in waist-high stacks like flower petals. Sitting at the center of it all, Duke Unalo Gerkolis quietly cursed the carelessness of his predecessor.

The archives were a complete disaster. Today marked the third day he'd spent, wasted really, trying to make sense of the room's contents. No matter how he tried, Unalo couldn't find even the slightest remnant of an organizational system. What exactly was the purpose of acquiring such a vast wealth in texts if every scroll was just as lost, in here, as before you found it?

Unalo felt his frustration rising and took a pause to let his blood settle. Perhaps he was being uncharitable. After all, Lord Blyton had no way to know that his castle was about to undergo a change of ownership. If he had, perhaps he would have invested some effort to tidy up the place.

Still, first thing tomorrow, Unalo resolved to send for an archivist from the city to tame the horrendous disaster that was his new collection. His patience exhausted, he stood up from the pile and brushed the dust from his knees, intent on finding a bottle of wine and a large glass. But as he took a step, he found his left foot had fallen asleep.

Unalo's arms pin-wheeled for balance as he fell backwards. The bookcase caught his fall, but teetering at the very top, a single wooden-handled scroll broke free and crashed painfully onto the crown of his skull.

He pressed a palm to check the wound. Crimson. "Perhaps a team of archivists," he muttered through gritted teeth. Unalo gave the offending scroll a contemptuous little kick, sending it skidding across the tile floor. The string holding it closed snapped, unfurling it like a flag in the wind. Bold, hard-edged text filled the exotic-looking parchment.

Although he wasn't fluent in their languages, Unalo recognized the work of dwarfish and elfish scribes. This was neither. The characters were sharp, almost dagger-like, yet flowed easily. His interest piqued, he grabbed up the scroll by its handles.

The parchment was quite dry and yellowed, even browning at the edges. Yet it was mostly intact, owing in no small measure to how thick it was. There was also a subtle pattern on the surface, almost like fish-scales. Unalo ran his fingertips across it to get a feel for the texture. It was as rough as a cat's tongue.

Whatever the scroll was, its origins lay far in the past. He'd heard stories from priests and clerics of the power of some of these scrolls from older times. Unalo scratched at the bump on his head and looked up to the top of the rack where the scroll had been perched. It may have taken months, perhaps years before his cataloging efforts had gotten that far. A shiver went through his skin. Was the scroll impatient to be found?

Having it translated would be tricky. The search for a scribe that could decipher it would draw attention to the scroll. Attention Unalo was interested in avoiding. Since the abrupt departure of the Gods, magical items were trading at a premium. There were rumors of priests and temples hoarding magical texts to maintain the illusion of divine connection in a bid to maintain their power.

If the scroll were half as exciting as Unalo hoped, news would undoubtedly spread, making it an enticing target for any one of a dozen interested parties. Keeping it secret would require generous amounts of silver. . . or steel. Still, his instincts told him it would be worth the investment. Unalo rolled the scroll back up and tucked it under an arm.

For now, there was other work to do. He still needed to take steps to secure his position as the new head of Lord Blyton's castle and its lands. The vassals would fall into line quickly enough. Sheep seldom take notice in a change of shepard.

His new landed peers, however, would be somewhat less convivial. Men of power didn't like reminders of their own mortality. They would test the strength of Unalo's grip, and soon. Should he falter and show weakness, they would swoop in and absorb his land into theirs. This was simply the history of things.

Unalo left the archives behind and swept into a drafty hallway, searching for another of his recent acquisitions, Holeck. Lord Blyton's long-serving Chief of Staff Holeck had developed a reputation for competence and efficiency. There were even rumors that Holick had almost singlehandedly held the castle together in Blyton's declining years.

If only he had taken a keener interest in the archives, Unalo thought sullenly. The sun had fallen below the horizon. He'd been in the archives far longer than he had intended. "Holeck," he called out. "Holeck!"

"Yes, My Lord?" The answer came from just over his shoulder. Unalo jumped halfway to the ceiling. He was not accustomed to being on the receiving end of surprises.

"How long have you been standing there?"

"I am always standing here, My Lord."

"In the hallway?"

Holeck's thin smile was only barely visible in the dim moonlight. "No, Sir, a step behind you. As is tradition."

Unalo wasn't sure if he felt reassured or threatened. Still, he would give his inherited Chief of Staff some leeway, for the time being.

"I have a scroll that needs translating, discretely. Your former lord must have acquired an impressive network of agents to build the archives as he did. Could any of them be used for this?"

"Certainly," Holeck answered instantly. "There are three capable linguists who owe the lord of this castle favors. I can have the scroll sent by a courier—"

"No, the scroll will remain here. I'm interested in the resources to translate it myself."

Holeck gazed into the ether. "So, you wish to have a scroll that you can't read, translated without anyone else seeing it."

"You see my quandary."

The older man nodded. "Some years ago, Lord Blyton had a particularly vexing book he had bought through a dealer in Aquabar. None of the scholars he approached could even identify the language, much less read it."

Unalo listened quietly, but his patience wore thin. "I assume you're not sharing this, only to tell me he never solved it."

"Of course not, My Lord. In fact, a royal archivist in Dawson heard of the problem and came to Lord Blyton with a solution. For a fairly healthy sum of gold, he agreed to sell a Scroll of Many Tongues."

Unalo snorted. The name brought to mind a rather peculiar image. "You're talking about some sort of translation spell, yes?"

"Yes. Activate it and any text in any language can be read, but only once."

"How fast is your quill, Holeck?"

"Quite fast, My Lord."

Unalo nodded. "Then once will be enough. Although such a spell scroll will fetch quite a premium today, with the temples hoarding everything magical."

"There may be an alternative for that as well, My Lord."

Unalo cocked an eyebrow. "Do tell."

Holeck's naturally gentle voice shrank to a conspiratorial whisper. "Not all of Lord Blyton's contacts were of an… academic persuasion. And not all of his archives were acquired with the full knowledge and consent of the original owners."

"You have an agent in mind to provide this service for me?"

Holeck gave a small bow. "Yes. He is very good at being places he should not, and finding things others prefer hidden."

"What is this shadow's name?"

"We know him only by his street-name; Grabber."

"How appropriate." Unalo absently rubbed at his goatee as he contemplated the next move. He had hired thieves and spies many times before in his rise to power. Several remained on retainer even at this moment. Such was a necessity for anyone with vision and ambition but denied the proper bloodline at birth.

A duke, even a self-appointed one, would need every capable agent they could hire, steal, or extort. Unalo saw an opportunity to test the quality of his predecessor's network.

"Very well, Holeck. Summon this 'Grabber' and I will see how he measures up."

"I'm afraid he will come up short, My Lord, on account of being a goblin."

The mighty walls of Central City filled Ansel's vision. They were higher than four tall men standing on each other's shoulders. The massive stone blocks fit together like puzzle pieces, leaving only a tiny strip of mortar between them. This stood in stark contrast to the rough clay-and-fieldstone walls the Deepspade's used to protect their vegetable garden from wild animals. Central City's masons were true craftsmen. Ansel hoped the trend extended to the local blacksmiths as well.

Yet despite the startling scale and precision of the wall, it had failed. Two gaping wounds had torn straight through, exposing the city's vitals. A swarm of men toiled to repair the damage, straining to reposition the giant stones using frames of timber and mile upon mile of rope.

Word of the great battles that had gripped Central City some months ago had reached even Ansel's remote farmstead but he could still hardly believe what he was seeing. An hour ago, he wouldn't have thought man could build walls so massive and strong. Now, he had to accept that there were forces powerful enough to tear them down. It was like taking a left-right punch from a tavern brawler.

Ansel knew in an abstract way that the world was a much bigger, grander place than what could be seen from the family farm, but he'd never had reason to apply the same logic to the world's evils. He shoved the unsettling realization to the back of his mind.

He came to the city's gates on foot. Stump was about a mile out of town, tied off to an oak tree big enough that not even a team of draft horses could uproot it. Hopefully, the fight would be worn out of him by the time Ansel returned.

The gate guards paid little mind as he passed through the great masonry archway leading inside the city. Ansel couldn't help but feel a little insulted by their disinterest in him, but in light of the breaches in the wall, he could understand why a dusty farm kid didn't grab their attention. Once inside the walls, his feet ground to a halt. Ahead, the claustrophobic grimy streets and alleyways that made up Central City loomed.

The sun was as high and hot as it had been in the fields. The narrow streets were stuffed beyond capacity with merchants, food stalls, people trading or eating lunch, wagons, horses, and the pungent aroma of all of them stewing together in the midday heat.

The village near his family farmstead had only one road, and you could see all of the shops, taverns, and churches without even turning your head. This was different. Ansel's eyes scanned for a blacksmith's shop, but the streets radiated out like the silk of a spider-web. They seemed endless. He could stumble around for a week without finding his brother's shop.

Overwhelmed, his father's advice rang through his head. Find a guardsman and ask for help. He spun around on a heel and tried to get the attention of one of the gate guards.

"Excuse me, good sir, but I've lost my bearings."

The shorter, thicker one craned his neck down to survey him. "Begone, whelp. We're on duty."

The taller one reached out and smacked his partner on the back of his head. "What's wrong with you, Mynor? Ain't you got any charity?" He looked down and regarded Ansel with a hospitable grin, even if it was short several teeth. "What can I do for you, young master?"

"I'm looking for my brother's forge, but I don't know where to start."

"A blacksmith, eh? What's your brother's name?"

"Tiklan, Sir."

"Tiklan? Can't say I know that one. Do you Mynor?" The portly guard shook his head, his jowls following a moment later.

"It isn't his forge... exactly," Ansel said. "He came to apprentice last year."

The kind guard nodded. "Oh, I see, I see. Well, that doesn't help then, he could be at any one of them." He scratched at his unshaven neck while he thought. "Tell you what, there are forges all over the city, but most of them are on Ash Avenue. Start there. Even if he's not there, one of the other smithies'll probably know who he's apprenticing with."

Ansel felt relieved. "Thank you, Sir. Truly. Where do I find Ash Avenue?"

The guards both laughed at the question. "Oh, you'll know it when you see it. Just follow the smoke."

Ansel thanked them again and wandered off, only slightly less confused, yet more hopeful than he'd been. There were still a dozen different streets ahead of him to pick from, some more appealing than others. Then he saw them; a dozen columns of smoke, some thick and black, some wispy and white, all reaching to join the clouds.

"Follow the smoke." He smiled and headed straight for the plumes. Well, as straight as the haphazard labyrinth of streets and footpaths would allow. His sandals pattered over rutted, cobblestone roads, through muddy alleys that smelled like freshly spread manure, past vendor stalls offering every conceivable type of food, dry goods, or service, several of which he was eager to learn more about, and several he wanted to run right the hell away from.

Despite the distractions, it wasn't long until Ansel had

found Ash Avenue. The guards were right; he knew it as soon as he saw it. Through either design or natural attrition, the shops on this smog-filled street were all of a kind. There were blacksmiths and weapon-smiths, tanners, woodworkers, meat-curers, papermakers, and potters. Every one of the trades represented on the street was hot, dirty, smelly, or smoky by their very nature. Some of them were all of these combined and more.

Ansel knew he was in the right place. He could almost sense his middle brother's patronizing look and quick hands. Tiklan was close by. He headed straight into the first forge he saw, and while he did not find Tiklan's master inside, the proprietor knew exactly which shop he was working for. Half a block later, he rapped his knuckles against the thick, ash-stained wooden door to Kelor's Ironworks and Implements.

When no one answered, he tugged experimentally at the handle. Locked. Ansel pressed his face against the grimy storefront window. What little light penetrated the soot on the glass revealed an eerie space, filled with great swooping blades, axes, and spades, hanging forebodingly from the walls and ceiling. Though Ansel knew they were more suited to turning dirt and harvesting wheat than felling men, the knowledge somehow failed to comfort him.

The storefront was closed, but perhaps there was someone in the back. He ducked into the alleyway to the side of the store, hoping to find a backdoor or window. Set high in the brick was a small, round portal. Char black soot rolled from it lazily, along with the muted grunts of effort and annoyance. Someone was home.

Ansel stood up on his toes to try and reach the window. "Hello? Is Tiklan in there?"

The grunting stopped abruptly. "Who's there?" The voice was strained, and sounded like ten miles of gravel road.

"My name is Ansel Deepspade. I'm just looking for my brother, Tiklan. Is he in there with you?"

Ansel heard something heavy clang onto a stone floor,

followed by a rush of footsteps. A door's hinges squeaked open around the back of the building, just out of his sight. Then a monster appeared in the alleyway. It was tall, with bulging forearms, biceps, and shoulders that could rend a boy in twain. It was black as a cave, except for the intense blue eyes, and it's ivory teeth bared in a snarl. The monster cried out and charged Ansel, locking him in its suffocating death-grip before his mind could react.

"Ansel!" it shouted. "You're here, you're really here!"

Ansel wiggled vainly against the vice holding him. Yet the voice had changed, shifted to something familiar. "Tiklan?!"

His brother released him and put his hands on Ansel's shoulders, looking him square in the eye. "Of course it's Tiklan? Who'd you think it was?"

"I, um… never mind. You look, ah, different."

Tiklan rubbed at his pitch colored forearms, but only succeeded in moving some soot around. "This stuff? I'm cleaning the chimney and bellows while Kelor's gone." Tiklan pointed at the big black smudges and handprints he'd just deposited on Ansel's tunic. "But look at this mess. You could have at least washed up before coming to see your favorite brother. Maybe wrung it out in a stream or something."

"Har-har, Tiklan. You're, um, stronger than I remember. And bigger."

"I've been swinging a five-pound hammer eight hours a day for a year. Even *you* would bulk up doing that. Come on, I'll give you the wood-token tour." He ushered Ansel through the back door and into the heart of the forge.

The walls in here were every bit as black as Tiklan's skin and clothes. The forge itself laid wide open, and the fire drawer below it had been pulled out to be emptied of cinders and ash.

But it was the giant stone wheel mounted to a timber frame that drew Ansel's attention. It looked like one of the wheels in the village millhouse. He pointed to it. "What is that?"

"That? That's my baby. Yup, I rigged it up myself two months ago. It took me almost six months to convince Kelor to let me build it."

"Okay. What is it?" Ansel asked again.

"Oh, it's a flywheel. It's hooked up to the bellows, you see? It keeps the airflow constant, which means the fire burns at a consistent temperature. Gives us better steel, and saves me a whole lot of work. Once it's going good, I can actually take a short break while it winds back down. Or Kelor can run the whole thing for a few minutes while I help a customer." Tiklan beamed with pride as he explained his innovation.

"That's interesting. Is your master coming back soon?"

"Why, you here to buy something?" Tiklan smiled down on his little brother, his ivory smile in bright contrast to his blackened face. Ansel couldn't help but shy away from the show of affection. Tiklan saw it and his smile faded. "You *are* here to buy something."

Ansel heard the pitch change in his brother's voice. He realized with some shock that he felt guilty. He'd gotten so used to hating Tiklan when they lived together, that this was new.

"I'm here to see you, too. The part was just a good excuse," he lied. "It's plowing season and I couldn't just leave without a reason."

Tiklan perked up a little at the explanation. "Oh, okay. Well, I'm not supposed to sell anything while Kelor's gone, said he didn't want me 'Giving away the forge for magic beans', whatever that's supposed to mean. What did you need?"

"A new ploughshare. I kinda' broke the last one."

His brother's head shook. "Hit a rock, huh? I told you to pick that field deeper."

"Yeah, well that doesn't help me now. When's this Kelor coming back?"

"Not 'till tomorrow morning, so we've got time to kill." Tiklan's eyes lit up like lanterns as an idea popped in his head. He grabbed Ansel by his wrist. "C'mon, I'm taking you to the *Blue Dragon*."

"What, like that?"

"Like what?"

"Tiklan, you look like a charcoal pit."

"Oh, right. I'll go wash up. Follow me; we'll clean up your tunic, too. You never know, we might run into some girls."

Barely an hour later, Ansel's legs strained to keep up with his brother, as Tiklan darted through the alleys, shortcuts, and tunnels of the city like a rat with a compass. His tunic was still damp from wash-water, and rapidly became still damper with sweat. They'd left Ash Avenue far behind, and traveled through several distinct sectors of the city, each with their own style, energy, and smells.

"Slow down, Tiklan, I don't know where you're going."

"We're just a block away. You're going to love it." Tiklan surged ahead and burst out onto a wide boulevard. Waves of horse-drawn carriages and delivery carts shot back and forth across the road like two mingling rivers. He stopped right at the edge of the rutted paving stones and watched.

"Wait for a gap." Tiklan didn't take his eyes off the carts whooshing by. For Ansel, the speed and the volume of movement were simply overwhelming. On the roads near their farmstead, you'd be lucky to see three carts pass in the same afternoon outside of harvest season. He could scarcely believe this many carts existed, much less that they were all in one place.

Tiklan reached back and grabbed Ansel's tunic. "Now!" With a quick jerk, Ansel found himself on the paving stones, horses and carriages clopping past him within inches.

"Go!" Tiklan gave him another yank, pulling them deeper into the maelstrom of hooves and wheels. A great gray and brown draft horse dodged out of the way, wrenching its cart to the side and costing the owner a handful of gourds, which tumbled over the side.

"Watch it, hayseed!" said the driver.

"Ignore him." Tiklan smiled. "We're halfway across, no point turning back now."

Ansel's face was white as fresh-picked cotton. "If you say so."

An ox-drawn wagon caused a bottleneck in the traffic as other drivers tried to flow around the lethargic animal. Tiklan took advantage of the lull to spring to the far side of the street. "C'mon!"

Ansel took a deep breath and, fighting the urge to close his eyes, sprinted for safety. He made it an entire stride before catching a foot on an uneven paving stone. The road rose up to meet Ansel, knocking the wind from his lungs. Through the bright spots bursting across his vision, he made out a horse turned on its side, galloping towards him most curiously. The animal reoriented in his mind's eye, and he realized that he was about to be trampled by a speeding cart.

He commanded his body to run, but his legs were sluggish to respond from the blow. Instinctively, he threw his arms over his head as the horse saw him. The animal reared up, while its back feet skidded across the stones. Then the momentum of the cart behind pushed against the animal's harness, knocking the horse forward.

Ansel watched as the horse's hoofs descended on him like a cave-in. As he tensed against the inevitable, two claws of iron sunk into his tunic and heaved him out of the way, just as steel horseshoes sparked against the pavestones.

Tiklan looked down at his little brother with a worried smile. "Are you hurt?"

Ansel looked around and realized that he was sitting on the far side of the street. The claws had been Tiklan's hands.

He pulled in a breath. "Uh, no, I don't think so."

Tiklan reached out a hand and tousled his hair. "You're fine, just a little rattled."

His arm swept wide, drawing Ansel's eye towards a carved wooden sign painted to look like a sapphire dragon of legend swooping down on a defenseless knight.

"We're here, and you look like you could use a drink."

Ansel struggled to his feet. "A drink? Tiklan, it's only past midday."

"Yeah, I know. We're getting a late start." Tiklan slapped him on the back. "I'll buy lunch."

Duke Unalo Gerkolis adjusted the chair behind his new desk. It was an administrator's desk with an irregular-shaped white marble top, supported by four oak pillars nearly as thick as the trunks they had been constructed from. The desktop had been smoothed and polished to a glass finish. It was embarrassingly expensive. At least it would have been, had Unalo been the one to pay for it.

The desk sat in an antechamber that had been converted into an office on Unalo's instruction. The castle's throne room was equally well appointed, however Unalo preferred the quiet of a private office. That, and there was still a certain untidiness in the throne room left over from the recent transfer of power. Several stains had proven quite resilient.

A soft rapping came at the door. Unalo set his quill down on the blotter and folded his hands.

"Enter."

A vertical line of light erupted from the middle of the double doors. Holeck, his Chief of Staff, glided through the opening. "Good afternoon, My Lord."

"What brings you, Holeck?"

"You asked me to inform you when Mr. Grabber had arrived to interview. He has just done so."

Unalo smiled broadly. "Excellent. Please, show him in."

"That won't be necessary." A squeaky voice echoed throughout the room, seemingly coming from everywhere and nowhere at the same time. Holeck's spine stiffened, while his eyes darted about in search of the source. Unalo wasted no time throwing open a draw built into one of the pillars of his desk and grabbing a small crossbow. A green-tinged sheen of poison suffused the bolt's tip.

"Show yourself," Unalo ordered calmly. In the far corner of the room, a shadow cast by one of the high-backed chairs set out for guests seemed to expand, then divide. The new shadow strode unhurriedly towards the chair, even as Unalo brought his crossbow to bear. As it approached, the shadow seemed to solidify. Its details resolved as it sat in the chair, until Unalo could clearly see a small, dagger-eared, shark-toothed creature looking back at him with a wide grim. Despite its size, every bit of the creature looked sharp. Even its large, golden eyes were adorned with pupils slit as if by stiletto blades.

"Grabber the Goblin, I presume?"

He opened his spindly arms wide. "Grabber will suffice."

Unalo lowered his crossbow, slowly, and set it on his desk between them. No longer a direct threat, but still within easy reach.

"Holeck, would you prepare two glasses of wine, please?"

The older man nodded deeply. "Very good, My Lord." He departed, closing the door behind him.

Unalo and his guest stared at each other for several long seconds. The goblin finally broke the silence.

"So, how's my audition going?"

"How long have you been in here?" Unalo asked coolly.

"Not long. Any secrets in your desk are safe, save for that poisoned crossbow, of course. I'm impressed; most men don't keep their heads that clear."

"I am not most men." Unalo brought up his hands and laced his fingers together. "Now that we're done impressing each other, may we get down to the purpose of this meeting?"

The goblin pointed at a long lobe. "I'm all ears."

Unalo smirked at the joke. "I have need of someone proficient in stealth and infiltration. Given your history of service with this castle, my chief of staff recommended you."

Grabber tilted his head ever so slightly. "Speaking of this castle, I seem to remember a different owner the last time I was here."

"There has been a change of ownership. Does that present a problem for you?"

"Not at all. I just want to know who's on top of the pile this month."

Unalo inclined his head ever so slightly. "This month?"

Grabber made a small throwing away gesture with a hand. "No offense, but I've already done jobs for three different masters of this castle, and we goblins don't live nearly as long as men do."

"Well, only time will tell." Unalo shrugged. "For now, I'm looking to hire a thief. Are you interested?"

"The gold will tell. What's the pinch?"

"I am looking for a magical item, specifically a Scroll of Many Tongues." Unalo kept his gaze steady and level, trying not to reveal anything to the stranger before him.

Grabber exhaled through his teeth, causing a dozen whistling sounds at once, like a choir of tiny songbirds. It was a most unsettling sound. "Gonna have to breach a temple for that. They've got some pretty serious wards in place these days."

"If it is beyond your scope, I can enquire after another."

The creature's pupil-slits dilated a fraction after the taunt. "Didn't say that did I, pink-skin? I can slip past the priests' wards. They're amateurs, dumping power into their spells, thinking a thicker wall will do the job better. But overstuffed spells can interfere with each other, leaves gaps."

"How big are these gaps?"

"Oh—" Grabber held a hand atop his head "—about yay big."

"I see. So what's your problem?"

"Not my problem, yours. The job will cost a thousand."

Unalo held his hands open. "A thousand silver is fair."

"Not silver. Gold."

Unalo's hands clapped back together. He sighed heavily, as though the offer had exhausted him. "Perhaps you are unfamiliar with the exact nature of my request. You see, people in my position hire thieves because they do not wish to pay fair market prices. You work as a sort of discount retailer. So, to be of value, and worth the risks, your fee needs to be markedly *less* than fair market prices, not double them."

Grabber snorted a laugh. "All right, then go buy one."

The two of them stared at each other across the white marble. Unalo tried to rush his thoughts further ahead. Grabber obviously knew that the scroll he was asking for couldn't be found on the open market, which also meant he knew magic items were being hoarded.

It was Unalo's turn to break the silence. "I concede the point. Still, a thousand gold pieces is a hefty sum for a solitary, single-use scroll. Five-hundred."

"Nine. I have a family to feed."

"Six-hundred gold pieces will fill a lot of mouths."

"You've obviously never seen a goblin brood patch. Eight-hundred."

"Six-fifty, with the promise of steady work if you succeed."

"Seven-hundred, *when* I succeed."

Unalo dipped his head, taking a moment to gaze at the swirling patterns in the marble of his new desk. His eyes returned to the goblin. "Done."

Grabber smiled brightly with his double rows of jagged ivory teeth. For a less traveled man, it would have been an unnerving sight. "I'll return with your scroll within the week. Pleasure doing business with you." He hopped down out of the high-backed chair and returned to the shadow. His outline blurred, until he seemed to dissolve into the dark like a clearing fog.

"But we haven't shared a toast yet," Unalo called out.

"Thank you, but no. Wine doesn't agree with us," came the reply from the room as a whole. A hollow quiet fell, and Unalo sensed that he was alone once more. A few moments passed before a knock came and the door creaked open. Holeck stepped in balancing a pair of stemmed glasses, filled halfway with rich red wine, perched atop a silver tray. He noticed the empty chair immediately.

"Our guest has departed?"

Unalo nodded. "It would appear so. Leave me a glass all the same."

"What shall I do with the other one, My Lord?"

"Drink it, of course."

Holeck gave a small bow. "Your grace is too generous."

"Not at all. Oh, and Holeck, have this room searched thoroughly for hidden doors, tunnels, etc."

"Very good, My Lord."

Ansel awoke to a most curious sight. As best as he could work out, an inexplicably animated hayfield was attacking him. He was about to comment on the implausibility of this, when several rows of hay stalks slapped him coarsely in the face.

"Ow!" In truth, the aggressive hayfield was the least of his problems. He also had a headache that felt like a tunneling project was being conducted through his brain.

"C'mon, get moving!" shouted the hayfield. That pulled Ansel back into the real world. An aggressive hayfield was one thing. A *talking* hayfield, however, was right out. He looked again through bloodshot eyes and realized that the rows of hay were actually bristles. Somebody was hitting him with a broom.

Oh, okay. That makes more sense, he thought hazily.

"Move it, kid. Gods, I thought you farmer types got up early."

Ansel tried to right himself, only to realize that his left leg wouldn't move.

"I think my leg's fallen asleep," he explained to the insistent, broom-wielding man.

"It's probably still drunk if it's anything like the rest of you."

Drunk? He took a moment to survey his surroundings; wood counter, thick stools, the smell of stale beer. A tavern.

The last dozen hours started to return in flashes. He and Tiklan had gone yesterday to the *Blue Dragon* and ate lunch, then had some ale, then some mead, then some rye whiskey. Judging by his current circumstances, they'd never left.

"Why does my head feel like somebody hollowed it out with an auger?"

"You don't know?" the exasperated barkeep asked. "That's Ale Penance. The Gods always build in consequences, Son."

"I want to die."

"Ha! Wait until you're older. You'll probably be fine by noon. Me, it could take days if I'd have drank that much."

"Where's my brother?"

"The smith's apprentice? He's out front praying to the weeds. Now crawl on outta here, kid. I have to clean up this place for the next round of idiots."

Ansel did as instructed. His leg had started to tingle, but he couldn't put any weight on it yet, so he hopped to the door, each step jarring through him and throbbing throughout his head.

He found Tiklan around the side, retching his malevolent stomach contents onto an unfortunate colony of thistles.

"Good morning, Tiklan." Ansel's voice had a slightly accusatory tone.

"Ah, you made it out alive. I'm glad." He assaulted the thistle again, and then wiped his mouth. "We should go back to the shop and get your ploughshare."

Tiklan finished his task then hobbled over and took Ansel's arm and threw it over his shoulder. He pointed them in a direction that Ansel assumed led back to Kelor's shop. Holding each other up like a shoddy bipod, they took a handful of steps before Ansel noticed his coin purse was missing.

"Wait, back to the door. I forgot my pouch."

Tiklan grunted but swayed back towards the door. Ansel trudged back up the steps on his still wobbly leg and tried to get the barkeep's attention. "Excuse me, Sir? I think I left my—" A little leather pouch arched through the air and smashed solidly into Ansel's face. "Thank you. And may I say you have excellent aim."

The barkeep grumbled and pointed to the street. Ansel picked up the pouch and rubbed his face, then resumed course with Tiklan.

"Well he's a cheery fellow."

"Who, Thad? He's not so bad. The other barkeep uses the fire poker to clear us out in the morning. Sometimes, it's still hot."

"You do this a lot?"

"Gods, no. I usually wait until the end of the week."

Ansel rolled his eyes, which somehow managed to hurt. Mercifully, the cross-street traffic was significantly reduced early in the morning, turned over instead to market stalls selling fruits, vegetables, breads, and meats from every corner of Beykla. Tiklan explained that by noon they would all be buttoned up again, and the rush of carts and wagons would resume.

The two brothers managed to wander back to Ash Street, which wasn't all that hard; one merely had to go in the direction from which well-dressed people were fleeing. They stumbled through the backdoor of Kelor's Ironworks and Implements and fell to the sooty floor in a heap.

"You're late, Apprentice." Kelor's ox-like frame loomed over them. "And paying an ale penance, by the looks of it."

Tiklan jumped up like a grasshopper. "Yes, Master. Sorry."

"What's this lump of gristle on the floor next to you?"

"That's my brother, Sir. Ansel. He came to town yesterday unexpectedly."

Kelor toed Ansel in the side. "Ansel, is it? Looks like he's been swallowed whole by a dragon and shat out again."

"That's closer to the truth than you might think, Sir."

Kelor nodded. "Been to see Thad, then. That'll do it. So, why's your inebriated little brother in my forge, Tiklan?"

Ansel propped himself up on an elbow and found his

voice. "Actually, Sir, I'm a customer. My father sent me to your shop specifically."

"Did he now?" Kelor offered him a hand up. Ansel accepted, only to have his shoulder nearly dislocated as the immense man yanked him to his feet. "Well, what can I do for old Yorick?"

Ansel clasped a hand to his shoulder and rubbed. "Well, we're having a problem going through ploughshares in the thick clay."

Tiklan snorted. "Yeah, the problem's a lazy rock-picker."

Ansel shot him a sour look, then turned back to Kelor. "Anyway, Father said the parts here wouldn't be so brittle."

"Well, he's right about that. You're in luck, Son. Come out front, I have something to show you."

Ansel followed the blacksmith as he lumbered into the storefront, the same one he'd seen through a window the day before. An ample selection of ploughshares hung from racks built into the ceiling. Most were various lengths of beaten iron, but one stood out from the rest. Its surface was smooth and polished like silver. It seemed to catch and reflect any light that got near it, almost drawing attention to itself.

Before he knew it, Ansel realized his hands were reaching up for the glimmering blade. He stopped himself and looked to Kelor for permission.

"By all means, pick it up. You have a good eye, lad."

Ansel lifted the share off the hook supporting it. While it had heft, it wasn't nearly as heavy as the one he'd broken two days ago. It was also much thinner, and sharper. One look and he knew he wouldn't want to get a foot caught under any plow it was mounted to.

"It's thin."

"Yes, it is," Kelor said. "It's made of battle-steel, so it can afford to be thinner than simple iron. And it will hold the edge much longer, even in the heavy clay of your region. The wood of the plow might well rot off before you have to sharpen that blade again."

Kelor's pitch was only half heard. Most of Ansel's attention was still lost on the ploughshare. He was drawn to his own reflection on its surface. Except it wasn't quite his reflection. He seemed taller, with a squarer jaw and broad shoulders. He looked mighty, noble.

Ansel shook his head. *Must be a distortion, a trick of the light,* he thought. Still, he knew this share was the right one for the Deepspade's farmstead. He turned to Kelor. "What are you asking for it?"

"Eight gold pieces."

Ansel grimaced. "My father only gave me five. Maybe one of the other—"

Kelor put up a hand. Strangely, only then did Ansel notice it was wrapped in a bandage. "Don't give up so quickly, little master. I can work with you. So, five gold, huh?"

"Yes." Ansel tossed him the pouch.

The smith caught it and hefted it in his hand. "Feels light." Kelor pulled the ties open and peered inside. "There's only two gold and some half silver pieces in here."

Ansel's face went slack. "What? Are you sure?"

"Here," Kelor held out the pouch. "Count it yourself."

Ansel leaned in. There was no denying, he was far short of the five gold he should have had. His spirits sank to plum new depths of despondency. He ran back into the forge and grabbed his brother by the shoulders. "Tiklan!"

"Whoa, Brother" Tiklan swayed unsteadily. "Not so loud, please."

"What happened to the gold?"

Tiklan looked up at him through red eyes. "You don't remember?"

"Obviously not, if I'm asking you!"

"We drank it, Ansel. You even bought the whole place a round."

Ansel threw his hands over his head. "Why'd you let me do that?"

"You didn't want to leave, and I assumed you had some

money set aside for food and drink."

Kelor appeared in the doorway, taking up most of it in the process. "Sounds like you're in a bit of a pickle, Son."

Ansel's headache seemed to rush in from all directions. Through the haze, he noticed that not only was Kelor's hand bandaged, but so too was his other forearm, and his right thigh. A red stain had seeped through the thigh dressing.

"What tried to eat you?"

The smith gave a dismissive little wave. "These scratches? They're nothing, just the result of working around so many sharp blades and pointy tools."

Ansel nodded politely, and decided not to mention how Tiklan seemed to be free of such injuries. "It seems two gold is all I have to offer, Sir. I think we should look at one of the other shares."

"Nonsense! Please, take it with my compliments."

"Really?"

"For the Deepspade clan? Of course. Your father's already given me a great apprentice, when he's not paying penance, the least I can do is cut him a deal on a lowly ploughshare."

"Oh, thank you, Sir. Thank you. This helps me more than you could know."

Kelor winked at him. "I think I have a pretty good idea. But do yourself a favor and tell your old man you paid the full five gold for it. We'll keep the real price our secret. Okay?" Ansel's head bobbed excitedly. "Good, c'mon, let me wrap it up for you. I wouldn't want you to get cut on the ride home."

Ansel walked with Kelor back out into the storefront. The smith lowered the share from the hanging rack almost gingerly, careful to grab it by the blunt spine, and held it at arm's length as though it might catch fire at any moment. For a moment, the mirrored surface seemed to track with Ansel, keeping his face in place even as it moved. As absurd as it sounded, Ansel thought for a second that the blade was *staring* at him.

Kelor walked briskly to the counter, threw the brown wrapping paper aside, and pulled out a skin of thick leather. He laid the ploughshare into the skin—edge pointed away from him—and rolled it up tightly. The smith bound the parcel with bailing twine in three places using knots more suited to the rigging of a sailing ship. Finally, for good measure, he reached inside his smock, removed his belt, and cinched it tight around the roll. Satisfied that the packaging was complete, he handed it over to its new owner.

As he took the impressively secured bundle, Ansel couldn't help but give the smith a peculiar look. "Um, thanks. I should go if I'm going to catch the noon barge."

"Too right you are. Shoo now, Ansel. Tell your father I'd be happy to take another of his boys on in a few years."

"I will." He leaned to shout into the forge. "It was good to see you, Tiklan. I'll come back to visit again soon."

A mumble that could nearly pass as a human sound came from the darkened room. As Ansel walked out into the morning light and marginally cleaner air, he looked back to the blacksmith's shop. Kelor stood in the doorway waving a farewell with one hand, while holding up his trousers with the other.

Father was right, he thought, *I don't understand things in the city.* He made his way towards the city gate, bid goodbye to the same thin and portly guards from the day before, and headed down the road. With any luck, Stump would still be tied to his tree, hungry and cross perhaps, but that would hardly deviate from his baseline disposition.

The rutted gravel road leading away from the barge had given way to the red clay trail that climbed over the three rolling hills leading directly to the Deepspade plot. Exhausted, a day late, and a little sunburned, Ansel was glad to see familiar terrain again.

His expedition to the city had been all the excitement he had hoped for, except in ways he hadn't expected. Tiklan was the most pleasant surprise of all. Two years ago, he would have been holding Ansel's head to the bottom of Stump's water basin. By the time he'd left Central City, Ansel was genuinely sorry to leave him behind.

Stump ambled on towards the homestead. They cleared the last hill, and Ansel saw the family house, out buildings, and half-plowed field in their entirety. It was only the third or fourth time he'd gotten this view in his entire life.

The city had suited him, Ansel thought, even if he only understood half of it. But home had it's own appeal. He spurred Stump forward, and within a few minutes they crossed into Deepspade territory. Elanir was waiting for him in the path; she must have seen him crest the hill.

"Do you have my shoes?" she asked impatiently.

Ansel shook his head solemnly. "I'm sorry, Itty, but the shoes were too big for you. You'll have to wait a few years for your feet to get longer."

Her too-short feet stamped in frustration. "That's not fair. They should make them for kids too!"

"I know, I tried to tell them that."

"Fine." Her mind changed gears. "Daddy says you're late."

"I know, Itty. I'll deal with Father. Go do your chores."

Elanir left in a huff, while Ansel dismounted and led Stump towards the shed. After tying him off and giving the mule his daily grain, Ansel untied the new ploughshare from the tack and carried it out to where Yorick was working in the vegetable garden.

"You're late," he said as Ansel approached. "I expected you back yesterday."

"I was, delayed. Kelor, that's the blacksmith, was out of the shop when I got there."

Yorick looked up and took measure of his youngest son. "You look rather well-traveled, Ansel. I'll assume Tiklan and yourself didn't let the opportunity go to waste?" Ansel's eyes were suddenly very interested in the tomato vine his father was tying off, or the pepper plants, or anywhere but Yorick's face. His father's head shook with a smirk. "As I thought, then."

Desperate to change the subject, Ansel held up the ploughshare. "I got the part, father, and it's a beauty."

Yorick took the package and inspected it quizzically. "Why is it tied off with a belt?"

"I'm not sure, maybe because it's so sharp. I think Kelor cut himself on it a couple times."

This raised Yorick's brow. "A clumsy blacksmith? I would think they would be weeded out during apprenticeship. Speaking of that, how is your brother?"

"Great. He's gotten lots bigger. And Kelor said he was a really good apprentice."

Yorick removed the belt and twine, then unfurled the leather covering the ploughshare. The noon sun shone off of the gleaming blade like a mirror. Yorick winced against the sudden brightness. He recognized the metal immediately.

"This is battle-steel."

Ansel's head bobbed proudly. "Yup, Kelor made it 'specially for the clay around here."

"Battle-steel is enormously expensive. How much did you pay for it?"

"Tw..." Ansel caught himself. "I mean, five gold pieces."

Yorick's head shook slowly in amazement. "You got a hell of a deal. The steel alone was worth that much. Well, I'll go fix it to the frame, then you and Stump will get back to work."

"Right now? I thought I'd have a little time to rest," Ansel pleaded.

"You did, yesterday. But since you're late, the field can't wait any longer."

Ansel opened his mouth to object, but realized the argument would be futile. "Yes, Sir."

"Good lad. Now go in the house and get something to eat while I fix this up. It shouldn't take half an hour."

Ansel shuffled dejectedly towards the house. He was about to pour himself a bowl of lukewarm potato soup when he heard expletives being thrown about outside with force and conviction. Yorick was not prone to cursing, so when Ansel heard him say; "Orc-shit! Felgon! and Dicermadon's Dong!" he went running for the shed.

He found his father sitting on the floor of the shed, the ploughshare lying next to him, and a small but steady flow of blood from a deep wound on his shin.

"Father! What happened?"

"The blade slipped and cut my leg while I was trying to secure it." Yorick tore a strip of cloth from his tunic's sleeve and wrapped the gash. "Don't worry, Ansel, it's not as bad as it looks. Go into the house and set the bone needle and fine sinew thread out on the table. I'll be along as soon as I get this cursed ploughshare in place."

Ansel couldn't help but be impressed by his father's toughness. He returned to the house and found the requested items, then ate his soup. His stomach was uneasy from the spill of blood he'd just seen, but three days on the road had left him very hungry regardless.

His father entered just as Ansel was washing out his bowl. "It's finished, and so too are you, I see. Hop out there and finish the field, please."

"Yes, Sir." Ansel left the house in a hurry, before Yorick could start stitching up his own leg. Stump was standing right where he'd been left. In a rare display of collaboration, Stump didn't try to squeeze Ansel against the wall while being fitted with the plow harness.

Within minutes, they were back at the spot in the field where they'd left off. The sun had also returned to its position, except inexplicably brighter. "Ya', Stump," Ansel called out. The mule obeyed, leisurely, and the plow jerked and dug into the heavy red soil. Immediately, Ansel noticed a difference with the new ploughshare. It bit in deeper, and was less prone to bucking out of the furrow. It sliced through the clay like a fine carving knife, which wasn't far from the truth.

Ansel responded by spurring Stump on, quickening the pace. Yet every time they went faster, the plow kept up. Before long, Stump was almost galloping through the field, kicking up a cloud of dust, while Ansel struggled to keep up and maintain a straight furrow. It seemed the plow simply couldn't be overwhelmed.

Ansel found he was actually enjoying it. He'd have the rest of the field done in an hour, so long as his legs could…

A sharp crack like thunder rang from the ground. The plow heaved up out of the soil and fell to its side, spilling Ansel onto the dirt. Another rock.

"Gods, no!" he pleaded. "Not again!" He scrambled to his feet and sprinted for the plow. To his amazement, the ploughshare was intact. Not even a scratch marred its polished surface. Confused, Ansel backtracked down the furrow and found a rock even bigger than the last one. Or, more specifically, *had* been a rock until very recently. Now, it was two rocks, perfectly cleaved through the center. The matching surfaces were smooth as glass.

From the house, Ansel heard his father shout. "Don't tell me you hit another rock!"

Ansel cupped his hands around his mouth. "Father, you have to come and see this!"

Learned Brother Jolis bid goodnight to the last students still awake and then locked the door behind him. The stars blazed invitingly in a cloudless sky, but his farseeing glass would stand alone tonight. It was the fourth day of Imbala, and by tradition the Temple's Study Sanctum must be occupied at all times by a Brother reading from a text completely new to them.

It was Feloe's way to challenge complacency. After two decades of constant study, it would be easy for Jolis or any of the more senior Brothers to grow comfortable in their knowledge and slow their pace of learning. Imbala combated this human failing.

Jolis gathered up his robe and sat down at the Desk of Insight at the center of the study. It was a small desk, large enough for only one text, a teapot and cup, and the four candelabras that slid into the corners. The size was meant to discourage clutter. Its wood was covered in an ancient patina of tea-rings and beeswax.

No one knew exactly how old the desk was, but it was agreed upon that it predated the Temple it resided in. There were even rumors that it had been used by Feloe himself, when he came down from on high to write *The Unrecorded Histories.*

From inside his robes, Jolis retrieved a flint to light the desk's four candles. As the years wore on, it was becoming harder to find a fresh text in the archives to read during

Imbala. Tonight's selection, for example, was a history of Kal-harkian glassblowing and terracotta pottery. It didn't promise to make for an exciting evening, despite the lithography.

He grabbed the teapot and a small, hot, green waterfall filled the waiting cup. Jolis settled into the small, hard chair which was designed to be somewhat uncomfortable to discourage dozing off and was about to begin his meditations, when a current of air whirled past the desk snuffing out all the candles. The wind gusted again, rattling the teapot and sending a candelabra skittering to the floor.

Jolis looked around the darkened room in confusion. The Study Sanctum was a sealed room; there were no windows to distract the brother's work.

"Is someone there?"

There was no reply. He fumbled about dumbly in the total darkness for several moments, trying to locate the flint set. Finally, his fingers located it and he relit a candle, and then touched it to the others. Jolis scanned the room for any sign of the source of the wind, but came up empty.

Curious, he thought quietly. The experience had rattled Jolis's nerves and his concentration. He took the teacup in hand and nearly drained its contents. The tea was still quite hot and he felt it course down his throat and settle into his stomach. Jolis sighed and returned to the book of pottery.

"Good evening, Learned Brother."

The squeaky voice came from directly behind his seat. Jolis spun around to get a look at the intruder. Perched atop a scroll tray sat a goblin wearing the distinctive saw-toothed smile of his race.

"This is a sanctum. How did you get in here?" Jolis demanded.

"Quietly," replied the goblin with practiced calm. "I must apologize to you, I had expected this room to be empty this evening."

A thief, then, Jolis thought. "You had the misfortune

of intruding during Imbala. This room will be occupied nonstop for weeks. Now be gone, thief, for Feloe knows how to protect his house."

The goblin cackled with laughter. "Forgive my good humor, Brother. Even if Feloe cared, he couldn't stop me from getting this far. Besides, I think we both know the Gods aren't answering our letters these days."

So, this demon knows of the Severance. I guess bluffing clerical spells is out, thought Jolis as he stood from the Desk of Insight and rose to his full height. "You are well-informed, thief, so I think it important that you know this. I have not always pursued knowledge as a Scholar of Feloe, and the knowledge I retain from my prior existence is of a martial nature."

The goblin snorted. "That was perhaps the most scholarly way someone has ever threatened to 'kick my ass.' It was beautiful, Brother. However, you should save your strength. I am here for an item, specifically a *Scroll of Many Tongues*, and you are going to show me where it is."

It was Jolis's turn to laugh. "And what leads you to believe I have any intention of doing that?"

"Because, dear Brother, I've poisoned your tea."

The bottom dropped out of Jolis's stomach, but he struggled to keep the shock off his face.

"You may already be feeling the effects. The tea seemed warm, almost like strong liquor, didn't it? I have the antidote, but don't delay. It is an impatient poison."

Jolis shook his head forcefully. "What you ask is impossible. This temple has only a handful of tongue scrolls left, and obviously you know there won't be anymore. Any one of my Brothers would die to protect them."

"How convenient, for I am willing to kill for one. Listen, Brother, your death won't save the scroll. I happen to know something of Imbala. Your vigil in here won't be disturbed. No one is going to come until morning. I will find the scroll by then and be gone with it. Remember, I *expected* to be alone."

The goblin held up a finger. "However, if you're willing to save a few hours of my time, I'm willing to save the remaining years of your life. Surely, you recognize that you are coming out ahead in this bargain?"

"We cannot afford to lose a scroll, it is too precious."

"You aren't listening. The scroll is already gone. The question you should be asking is if your order can afford to lose a Brother of your seniority, in *addition* to the scroll."

Jolis held his head high in defiance, but then the room started listing to one side. He tried to right himself, but stumbled and had to catch a hand on the desk.

"As I said, impatient," said the intruder. "Just tell me where the scroll is and you'll be right as rain within the hour. Then, you can get back to reading your pottery book."

Jolis lashed out. "Don't mock the Imbala, heathen!"

"My apologies. Where is the scroll?"

The Brother resisted, but what little color he could see from the candlelight started to fade from his sight. The walls began to heave as though they were breathing.

"I can see you're starting to hallucinate. There is still time to take the antidote, but it grows short. Just point me towards what I need and you'll live long enough to chase me down."

Jolis smiled thinly at the offer. In his current state, it even held some appeal. Most importantly, however, he knew the thief's words were true. The scroll he was looking for was no more than three arm-spans from where the goblin sat. Given a few uninterrupted hours, he would have it in hand, and no witnesses to his crime would survive to give testimony.

"All right thief," Jolis said with resignation. "You win."

"No, Brother, we both win. Guide me."

Jolis held up an unsteady hand and pointed at the third bookcase in from the wall. "Find *Odeast's Trieste on The Hidden Treasures of Adoria*."

"Ha! Subtle." The goblin hopped down from the scroll tray and went to the bookcase as directed. His thin fingers and sharp claws danced over the titles. He even appeared to understand the order's labyrinth cataloging system like an experience archivist. The thief's finger rested on the cover of Odeast in less than a minute. He looked back at Jolis, awaiting further instruction.

"Remove it."

The intruder pulled out the book. A minute but audible *click* emanated from the wall behind the bookcase. Without being told, the goblin pulled on one side of the case, then tried the other. The heavy case swung open easily on perfectly balanced hinges, exposing a vault of scrolls, amulets, potions, and magical armors. His large, gold eyes lit up like torches.

"Be not greedy, thief. Take what you came for and no more."

"Don't worry, Brother; I didn't bring a bag." The intruder disappeared into the vault. He reappeared a moment later, holding a small scroll of a dark velum. He held it into the light with a noticeable look of disgust contorting his already alien face.

"Is this made out of cured tongues?"

Despite the poison wreaking havoc with his senses, Jolis couldn't help but laugh at the goblin's discomfort. "It isn't called a *Scroll of Many Tongues* for nothing, thief. Now, the antidote."

The goblin regarded him with a bow. "That was the deal. The antidote is in the teapot. You'll have to drink the entire thing."

Jolis turned and drunkenly dove for the teapot. He threw the lid to the floor, shattering the porcelain against the tile. He sucked down the hot tea greedily, burning the roof of his mouth and throat in the process as it drained into his stomach. He had larger issues than a burnt palate.

"Good," said the goblin. "Now, I warn you, the antidote is itself nasty stuff. You will probably pass out, and drinking that much tea all at once, odds are you will have passed water before you awaken. I'm sorry I can't save you from that indignity, but you'll be alive."

"I would thank you, but for the fact you were the cause in the first place." Jolis's burnt tongue muddled his words, but he made himself heard.

The goblin shrugged. "We all have our calling, Brother. I'm sorry ours had to be at odds this night. Goodbye."

"Goodnight, thief. Not goodbye. I will see you again."

The goblin smiled at the challenge. "Goodnight, then." With that, he tucked the scroll under an arm, just in time for Jolis to succumb to the antidote. His vision was overcome with black as he fell to the floor.

Grabber snuck back out of the temple through the same warding interference that had granted him entry. The night was moonless, as he'd planned. Even if he had been discovered during his exit, any pursuers would have to combat the near pitch-black landscape, while he could see quite well.

He spared a thought for the brother he'd left behind in the study. He'd lied, of course. The teapot hadn't contained antidote, but the rest of the poison Grabber had brought. Unless the Brother had the constitution of a dragon, he would never awaken.

It was the right thing to do, Grabber realized. Leaving witnesses was… sloppy, especially ones who could identify him by face and voice. So, he'd lied. Giving the Brother hope for the antidote prevented any final nothing-to-lose heroics and kept everything nice and civil.

Still, Grabber had felt a pang of remorse that the Brother wouldn't have the opportunity to track him down. Perhaps it was simply respect for another being dedicated to their chosen path. Perhaps it was guilt for leading a man to his death with false promises.

Neither possibility was a healthy one for someone in his

profession. Grabber shook the thoughts from his mind. Gold was a thief's only attachment; sentimentality got people captured or killed.

Clear of the temple and with no signs of pursuit, the stealthy goblin reached the tree line and vanished.

It is a constant; that the smaller an area's population, the faster news travels through it. By the end of the week, everyone had heard of Ansel Deepspade and his phenomenally fast plow. Neighboring farms rented him and Stump out to till their fields. Many of them just asked to borrow the plow itself, but Yorick forbade it. He might lose his son's use as a farmhand for a day, but there was no way he would trust a covetous neighbor with the plow unsupervised. The extra income for the farm didn't hurt either.

Ansel was working the Lorian's fields, tilling behind Stump at just short of a dead run, when a passing wagon spotted him and rolled up to a stop. He was concentrating so hard on keeping the furrow straight and true, that Ansel didn't notice the man waving his arms until he reached the end of the field and he had to turn around.

"Whoa there, young man!" said the stranger. "I wish a word with you."

Ansel wiped the sweat from his forehead and put up a hand against the sun. Upon closer inspection, the frantically waving man looked familiar. He decided to give Stump a rest and walked towards the road.

"What can I do for you, Sir?"

"Nothing, my lad. I wished to offer you something," said the widely smiling face.

As Ansel came closer, he was able to place the face. The

bulbous red nose and pitted, perpetually blushing cheeks belonged to Mr. Vitolo. He was, among other things, the chairman and organizer of the annual Summer Solstice Festival that Lord Blyton hosted at his castle. His father had taken the family to such a festival when he was younger, before Elanir had been born and his mother was still alive. It was a bittersweet memory.

"What's that, Sir?" he asked politely.

"I was just passing by when I saw your mule and plow moving at an incredulous speed. At first, I'd assumed you'd lost control of him and were in danger. Naturally, I stopped to try and help. But then I realized the field was in good order and you were in full command. That's astounding, my boy!"

"It's nothing, I've got a good plowshare. The amazing part is that Stump keeps working so hard."

"Stump?" Ansel pointed a thumb back at the mule. "Ah, clever. You are too modest, Son. What's your name?"

"Ansel Deepspade, Sir."

"Yorick's boy?"

He nodded. "Yes, Sir."

"Well, Ansel, I'd like to invite you and your mule to the Summer Solstice Festival, where you'll compete in the plowing competition. You may have a real chance at knocking out the reigning champ."

"Who's that?"

"He goes by Caballus, and he's won the plowing competition the last seven years, not to mention the jousting competition and the ale-drinking title."

"I don't know, Sir. He sounds like a tough man."

"Well, he's certainly tough. But listen, young Deepspade, people love an underdog, and nobody likes watching a sport where the winner is a forgone conclusion. It takes away all the excitement. C'mon, it'll be a big honor for your family."

"I don't know, I'll have to talk to my father."

"Of course, of course. And make sure to tell him this will be the biggest Solstice Festival in years. There's a new duke in the castle, and he's looking to make a grand entrance."

This was news to Ansel. "What happened to Lord Blyton?"

Mr. Vitolo leaned down to whisper in Ansel's ear. "It's best not to dwell on such questions, my lad."

"Oh. Well, who's this new duke, then?"

"Someone calling himself Gerkolis. But that's hardly important. All we need to know is he's introducing himself at this festival and wants to make a memorable impression."

Ansel considered this for a moment. "Tell you what; I'm almost done with this field. If you can wait about an hour, you can follow me back to the house and talk to my father."

"Capital idea, my boy. I'm sure old Yorick will be pleased as a peach to see his son compete."

Mr. Vitolo's prediction proved accurate. Back at the Deepspade farmstead, Yorick's smile dispersed any lingering doubts Ansel had.

"Do you really think he could beat Caballus?"

"Indeed I do, Yorick. I'm not in the business of leading lambs to slaughter. It's my job to put on a good show for the people. Ansel and Stump can give them one."

"Good. Never did get on with Caballus."

"You know him, Father?" Ansel said.

"Yes, I do. Better than I'd like to."

"Why's that?"

Yorick crossed his thick arms over his chest. "Well, you didn't hear it from me, but he can be a real horse's ass."

Mr. Vitolo found this surprisingly hilarious, and took a few moments to regain his composure.

"Couldn't have said it better myself, Mister Deepspade. Too bad Ansel here couldn't take him on for the ale-swilling trophy too. That would really twist his tail."

Yorick shot his boy a sideways glance. "I think he's had enough training for that event for one year."

"So he has your blessing, then?"

Yorick nodded deeply. "He'll be there."

"I've secured another six acts for the courtyard, including one of those blokes who juggles flaming knives. And that's not all, My Lord..."

The silence in Unalo's office stretched out like a tensed bowstring. A few uncomfortable moments lapsed before he realized the ruddy-faced promoter sitting across his desk was waiting for him to respond. Unalo wondered what would happen if he didn't say anything. How long would the man wait for a signal to proceed? Or would he simply wait indefinitely, finally expiring from dehydration?

Unalo decided, reluctantly, that it wasn't worth the risk. "There's still more, Mister Vitolo? Please, do go on."

"Thank you. The other day I found a young man who can dig a furrow fast as lightning. He'll be the perfect dark horse competitor for the plow race."

"An ironic choice of phrase, considering the defending champion." Unalo's wit was rewarded by a rather dim stare from the red-nosed man. "Dark horse, I was referring to... on account of him being a…"

"Oh, I see now." He smiled a wide black-toothed grin. "Too sly you are, My Lord. Too sly."

Not for the first time since sitting down with Mister Vitolo, Unalo wondered exactly where it had all gone wrong. During his years of plots and scheming, he'd always known that lordship would come with its own set of mundane duties. However, wasted afternoons planning for the droll minutia of every dull serf festival hadn't been among his imaginings.

These frivolities seemed to happen at least every other week during a slow month. It was a wonder anyone found time to plant crops at all. Still, even commoners had appetites that must be kept sated. Keeping them drunk on cheap mead and entertained by third-rate drifters with delusions of talent twice a month was better than the alternatives, which usually involved pitchforks, torches, and unruly mobs.

Just as Mister Vitolo was about to launch into his next diatribe on the importance of hiring quality fried hog skin vendors, the office door opened and Holeck came to the rescue.

"My Lord, forgive the *short* notice, however the guest we've been expecting arrived a moment ago."

Unalo nodded. His Chief of Staff's emphasis on 'short' could only mean that Grabber, the goblin thief, had returned from his task. Unalo stood up from his chair and tried to hurry the bulbous promoter from his office.

"Thank you, Mister Vitolo, it sounds as though you have the Summer Solstice Festival under control."

Vitolo's eyes went wide. "But, we haven't ironed out the rules for the toad stomping contest yet!"

For the barest moment, Unalo was tempted to ask why the mass execution of defenseless amphibians could possibly require a formalized rule structure, but decided against it.

"I have every confidence that you'll riddle it out, Mister Vitolo. Now, I won't take up any more of your time. I can clearly see that you have the situation well in hand. Good day to you."

Holeck moved into the office and put a hand on Vitolo's shoulder, then gently but firmly moved him towards the exit. The door clicked shut, and Unalo turned his head to regard the shadow in the far side of the room.

"I presume you are already here. Isn't that right, Grabber?"

The shadow stirred and then a short sharp creature came forth from its folds. "Indeed, My Lord."

"I further presume that you wouldn't have returned without the item."

The pale green goblin reached for a pack slung over his shoulder and pulled out a tightly wrapped, dark brown scroll. Unalo's pupils swelled to saucers at the sight. Grabber sliced through the binding with a sharp claw and the scroll unfurled across the desk.

Unalo leaned over to inspect the acquisition more closely. It wasn't long before his eyes recognized the macabre pattern in the strips of leather. He let the discovery pass without comment.

Unalo looked up to the goblin's large, nocturnal eyes. "Where did you find it?"

Grabber gave a small smirk. "Now, now, My Lord. I can't be giving away my favorite hoards. It would be bad for business."

"Fair enough, but you're certain it's genuine?"

"Yes," he said, "unless they went to all that trouble to hide a worthless fake. Not delivering what the client demands is also bad for business."

"As is being too trusting." Unalo pressed a soundstone on the side of his desk. Holeck wore its mate on a necklace.

"Yes, Lord?" came Holeck's inquisitive voice.

"Please recover the scroll I've set aside for translation, and bring a quill and clean paper."

"Straight away, My Lord. Just as soon as I can get Mister Vitolo to stop pawing at the tapestries."

"Very well." He touched the soundstone again and it fell silent. "If you don't mind, I'd like to see the scroll work for myself. If all is as you say, then you will be paid your seven hundred gold."

"The agreement was seven fifty," Grabber said firmly.

Unalo only smiled. "You are trying to steal fifty gold coins from me, goblin. While I respect the dedication to your craft, it will not work in this case. Seven hundred was our agreement. I keep careful records of all my dealings."

It was Grabber's turn to smile. "Documentation carries its own risks. I'm sure there are any number of people who would be very interested in reading your records."

"That would prove difficult without the proper cypher. Do you object to having your merchandise verified?"

Grabber shook his head. "Not at all. I find it amusing, in fact. I've had dealings with this castle for years without complaint."

"This castle, yes. With me, no. Trust takes time to earn, Grabber; and no offense intended, but with a thief it will naturally take longer still."

The door opened abruptly. Holeck's reappearance diffused the rising tension. "I have the scroll, My Lord."

"Excellent." Unalo motioned for his Chief of Staff to approach. "Please, sit down and ready your quill."

Holeck set the mystery scroll on the desktop and found a chair. Unalo took the frail, ancient parchment and delicately unrolled it. The smell of dust and dry leather filled the air, but the strange, stiletto shaped characters were just as unintelligible as they had been before. He tried turning it around, in case he had been viewing it upside down. No luck.

He looked to Grabber. "How is the translation scroll activated?"

The goblin only shrugged. "The man I took it from was not forthcoming."

"It's hardly worth seven hundred gold as a desk ornament."

"Perhaps not, but that's what you will pay. Our agreement was to provide the scroll, I've done so. Using it is your problem."

With a flurry of frustration, Unalo threw the wooden-handled scroll onto the desk and thrust a finger at the thief. Just as he was about to string together an impressive line of expletives questioning the legitimacy of the goblin's heredity, something caught his eye and gave him pause. The ancient parchment had fallen onto the *Scroll of Many Tongues* at an angle. Where the two overlapped, the dagger-like characters seemed to bleed and morph before his eyes. After a moment, familiar words formed on the page.

He quickly straightened the parchment so that both documents overlapped completely. "Holeck, your quill."

The older man sat bolt upright, paper in hand and quill and inkwell waiting to transcribe whatever came next. "I am prepared."

With growing avarice, Unalo's gaze fell to the first line. He began...

In the time of Abandonment, there will come many portents.

A man of humble blood rises as the sun, with brilliance from the East.

His ascension will be shadowed by a relic from the past, reborn to a new age, yet hidden in plain sight.

If wielded by a deft hand, it will slash through the very strings of fate, freeing the deserving to chart their own destiny.

Unalo looked up from the dry parchment and at his Chief of Staff. Holeck had a fast hand. He finished transcribing only a moment after Unalo finished speaking.

"Do you have all of it?"

"Yes, My Lord. Is there more?"

"Yes, lots mo..." As his eyes returned to the scroll, Unalo realized the characters were returning to their original, incomprehensible state. His jaw nearly hit the desk. "What's happening? Why has it stopped working?"

"It's a single use scroll," Grabber said. "Maybe it thought you had finished."

"I merely paused!"

Holeck set down his quill. "Perhaps it wasn't the brightest scroll on the shelf."

Unalo's teeth ground as he contemplated spending seven hundred gold coins on a single quatrain of text. Still, perhaps it was not a total loss.

"Please read the text back to me."

Holeck did so, and Unalo felt his mood brighten line by line. The time of Abandonment certainly fit the recent severance from the Gods the priests were wailing on about. Also, it wasn't difficult to insert himself as a man of humble blood rising in the East, and taking charge of his own destiny held a certain appeal.

"Grabber, I have a new assignment for you."

The Deepspade family continued on with a purpose through the rowdy sights and sounds offered by the Solstice Festival. The party had gotten underway the day before. Half the countryside had gathered to take in all the performances, sporting events, and gastronomic atrocities on hand.

Elanir bounded around the cart, pointing at a female performer spinning atop a spear set into a turntable. Then she was on the other side screaming about a man eating a flaming sword.

"That's enough for now, Elanir," said her father. "We can see them just as well as you can."

She pointed emphatically. "But Daddy, that man's eating fire!"

Ansel rolled his eyes. "It's just a trick, Itty."

"How's he doing it, then?"

Ansel was caught flatfooted. He cast about his brain for a passable answer. "Simple. He's lined his throat with cotton."

It was the best he could come up with on the spot. Apparently, it was good enough for a seven year old. Elanir, who nodded sagely. "Ah. Tricky devil."

Yorick led Stump through the tangle of half inebriated people and towards the makeshift arena in the castle's courtyard. Ansel's palms started to sweat as he pulled the tarp off his plow. Outside of rock-skipping on the river with his brothers, he'd never competed for anything in his life.

His anxiety built as the field came into view.

Farm hands stooped over the soil, raking and shoveling a layer of… something... into piles, which were then put onto carts and hauled off. One of the carts passed them, and Ansel realized it was filled with hundreds of smashed toad carcasses.

"Shame to waste the legs," Yorick said. "Fry them up in a little olive oil, they make a fine meal."

Elanir's face contorted in revulsion. "Yuck, Daddy. That's disgusting."

Ansel had to agree, but kept his eyes towards the field. Other contestants had already arrived and worried over their plows, harnesses, and beast of burden. Some had brought enormous draft horses, twice the size of Stump. Others preferred oxen, whose massive shoulder muscles bulged a foot above their backs.

His stomach started doing flips. Magical ploughshare or not, he and Stump were going to get tilled under like last year's wheat stalks.

The cart rolled to a stop, and Yorick motioned for Ansel to help him unload the plow. Elanir, being a precocious little girl unacquainted with social boundaries, immediately set about introducing herself to everyone in sight.

"And that's my big brother, Ansel." She pointed at him while talking to a group of disinterested farmers. "He's here for the plowing competition, which he's gunna win, 'cause he's the fastest plow alive."

This elicited a few sideways glances in Ansel's direction. However, after a cursory examination, the farmers shared a chuckle.

Elanir put her hands on her hips. "What's so funny?"

A man in a wide brimmed straw hat regarded her with a patronizing, coffee-stained grin. "Nothing, little one. We didn't mean to laugh. I'm sure your brother is plenty fast, but you've never seen the likes of Caballus. We're all lucky just to lose to him. Your brother and that donkey will be lucky not to get trampled."

"He's a mule, and we'll just see, won't we?" she insisted.

Ansel finished heaving the plow onto the ground and went to retrieve his little sister. "All right, Itty, I think you've made enough new friends for now."

"But they laughed at you. That's rude!"

Ansel put a hand between her shoulders and nudged Elanir back towards the cart. "Maybe they know something we don't. C'mon."

By then, Yorick had pulled the tarp off the family's plow. The shimmering blade caught not only the light of the noon sun, but the eyes of most of the rest of the competitors. He turned down several offers for the plow over the next hour.

With the remains of the toad cleansing finally shuttled away, the grounds were readied for the plowing contest. Crowds of spectators had started to gather. The competitors milled about in the afternoon heat, oiling leather harnesses, polishing brass, and taunting one another. Ansel busied himself grooming Stump's mane and tail.

The sounds of a commotion came from the field's entrance. Great heavy hoof falls like that of a charging warhorse filled the air. Ansel looked for the source and saw an enormously broad, bare-chested man at the head of a cloud of dust. Although he couldn't see it yet, the newcomer's horse must have been twelve hands high.

Cheers erupted from the crowd. Clearly, the new arrival was not a stranger to them. His stead skidded to a stop amid an obscuring haze of dust, while the crowd started chanting. Ansel couldn't make it out at first, but then the name became clear. Caballus. The crowd was welcoming their champion.

The clearing dust had another surprise to reveal. Ansel was dumbfounded by what he saw. As his mind tried to work out what he was seeing, Elanir summed up the situation simply.

"He has a horse for a butt."

Indeed, that was the case, for Caballus was a centaur. Ansel had heard only wild stories of them, tales told by travelers from far-away lands, brimming with exotic peoples and dangerous beasts. Looking at him, Ansel wasn't sure which category to file Caballus under. The horse-man pulled his own two-wheeled cart and plow with an elaborately fringed leather harness.

"I don't suppose I could recruit a few strong men to unpack my plow?" bellowed Caballus's voice. In seconds, a dozen fans clamored and fought their way up the cart to unload the heavy plow. Caballus scanned the crowd approvingly, when someone caught his eye.

"Do my eyes deceive me, or is that old Yorick Deepspade?"

"It is," Ansel's father said. "And you're fashionably late, I see."

Caballus unhooked himself from the cart and trotted over. "Builds suspense, you know how it is. So, are you here to cheer on an old friend."

"Not precisely."

The centaur feigned shock. "Don't tell me you're crazy enough to compete."

"Of course not, don't be absurd. I'm not fool enough to challenge the great Caballus. My son, Ansel, on the other hand…"

"Ha! Where is this brave boy? I'd like to meet him."

Yorick waved for Ansel to come over. Reluctantly, he obliged.

"Son, this is Caballus."

Remembering his manners, Ansel offered his hand, although at a considerable upward angle. "Pleased to meet you, Sir."

The horse-man clamped down on Ansel's palm and shook it like a terrier with a rat. "And I, you. Good luck digging into the field today."

"Thank you, Sir."

To their right, a familiar face mounted the official platform and addressed the crowd with a bullhorn.

"Welcome good people!" Vitolo's voice boomed. "The

plowing competition is about to commence. But first, our generous host would like to say a few words. So without further ado, please welcome our lord, Duke Gerkolis!" He swept aside among a smattering of applause, only to be replaced by a man of modest stature dressed in silken finery.

He took a moment to collect himself before speaking. Ansel was struck by the duke's apparent youth. Certainly Gerkolis was older than he, but his skin was quite smooth, and his hair devoid of gray.

"Good afternoon, my people, and thank you for making the journey here today. Please, enjoy all the pleasures, excitements, and distractions the festival has to offer. Consider my hospitality as a simple repayment for your hard work; because without cooperation, there is no prosperity for any of us."

The crowd responded with practiced enthusiasm.

"You are too kind. Now, let the…" The duke turned towards Vitolo, who whispered an answer in his ear. "… Plowing competition begin without delay!"

The mix of spectators and competitors returned their attentions to the field. The duke returned to the covered throne reserved for him atop the platform, while Mister Vitolo came down the stairs holding a sheet. He headed straight for the centaur.

"Good day, Caballus. Are you ready for the first heat of the afternoon?"

The champion gave a dismissive laugh. "Always. What's the first match?"

Vitolo took a moment to consult his sheet. "Ansel Deepspade vs. Caballus."

Ansel, who was still within earshot, erupted. "What! But I haven't even had a practice run yet, and you're already throwing me up against the six time champion?"

"Seven time," the centaur corrected helpfully.

"Whatever!"

Mister Vitolo was unmoved. "Sorry, Son. But the heats are

determined alphabetically, and it just so happens there's no one entered between 'A' and 'C' this year."

"Yeah, but alphabetical's supposed to go by surname," Ansel struggled. "Everybody knows that."

"Oh, but of course you're right. In that case, the first match is…" Vitolo glanced at the sheet again, "Caballus vs. Deepspade, Ansel. Now stop procrastinating and get your rig setup. The match starts in five minutes." With that he tottered off, preceded by his bulbous red nose.

Caballus looked down to where Ansel stood. "That was a cruel thing he did. I don't envy the way you're going to have to start your career. I have no plans to embarrass you though, so don't worry about that."

Yorick put a hand on Ansel's shoulder. "Come, Son, we have work to do."

They spent the few minutes they had, feverishly preparing Stump and the plow for what was to come. Just as Yorick tightened the final harness strap a horn sounded, signaling the first two competitors to take their places.

With the obvious dread of a man walking towards the gallows, Ansel prodded Stump towards the starting line. The field was divided in half, with the starting stations on the far corners of one side. Caballus was already in place. He regarded Ansel with a small, respectful bow.

Ansel nodded in return and took a moment to observe his opponent's rig. The plow was weighted down with a large wooden box of ballast. Without a plow driver, Caballus still needed to weight down the plow's frame to make sure the blade dug into the dirt properly. In addition to the ballast, there was an extra strap attached to a strange armature on the coulter and running to Caballus's right hand.

That's how he controls the pitch of the ploughshare, Ansel thought. *Clever.*

The horn sounded from the official platform again, followed by Vitolo's thundering voice. The bullhorn was really not needed, with a set of lungs like his.

"A quick review of the rules. Each plowman has been given one half of the field to till. Each plot must be cut into ten even furrows. No more or fewer. Fields will be judged on both time and quality of the rows plowed. Now, on the sound of the horn, the contest will commence."

His palms already slick with sweat, Ansel gripped the leather of Stump's reigns even tighter in anticipation of the horn. He didn't have to wait long. The tone rang out, rich and true. Ansel snapped the reigns as though they were whips. In response, Stump took off with all the power and speed of a tortoise suffering Ale Penance. Clearly, Ansel had failed to properly express upon Stump the urgency of the situation.

On the far side of the field, Caballus suffered from no such miscommunication. He charged forward with purpose, straining against the harness lashed across his... pelvis, chest? Whatever, the horsey bit up front. Leather creaked under the tension.

The noise from the crowd surged in response to their champion's early lead. Only the lone voice of his father urged Ansel forward. It seemed a lost cause however; he didn't have any fruit to spurn Stump forward with.

"Yah, Stump!" Ansel cracked the reigns again. "Yah!"

Ansel looked over his shoulder at his competition. Caballus had nearly reached the end of his first row. "We're going to lose. Is that what you want?"

His anxiety supplanted with anger, Ansel tried to will the plow forward without Stump's assistance. Much to his surprise, it obliged him. The plow surged forward, putting slack in the reigns and striking the mule in the flanks with the frame. Stump panicked and broke into a one-mule stampede.

Ansel had to break into a dead run to keep up with the retreating plow. His feet blurred under him as Stump's hooves kicked dirt and dust into his face. The plow rocked wildly, confounding his frantic attempts to steady it and keep the furrow straight.

Caballus had completed his first turn and was working his way into the second row, but Ansel was gaining ground. Realizing that they might actually have a race on their hands, the noise coming from the crowd redoubled. Yorick's thin voice was downed out, but Ansel was already committed. He didn't dare slow down for fear of being dragged by the reigns wrapped around his hands.

The first lane was over almost before Ansel realized it, yet Stump still charged ahead heedlessly. He had to slow the mule somehow to make the turn. Ansel pulled back on the reigns as hard as he dared, cutting the bit into Stump's lower jaw.

"Whoa, Stump!" The mule slowed a fraction, but not enough. Ansel pulled hard to the left, trying to make the turn, but they were still moving too fast. Stump managed to pivot almost around his own center to avoid stumbling out of the field. But the quick change of direction whipped the plow, and Ansel, around like a lash. He tumbled to the dirt as the plow fell to its side.

A gasp cried out from the crowd, but as soon as it was apparent that Ansel was unharmed, their feigned concern turned to laughter. Ignoring them, he jumped back to his feet. The muscles of his arms bulged as he strained to right the heavy plow.

Back in position, he gripped the leather reigns again and snapped hard.

"Yah, Stump!"

For once, Stump listened. Caballus had again widened his lead as a result of the crash. He was starting his third row, and showed no signs of slowing. Clouds of dust from the two plows choked the air as Ansel ran to keep up with his rig. The ploughshare sliced through the dirt with ease, almost singing as it parted the earth.

Ansel and Stump found their pace. It was brutal, but manageable. More importantly, it was faster than Caballus. The only question was if enough time remained to close the gap. The roar of the crowd had returned, even Duke Gerkolis had risen from his throne to get a better view as the battle unfolded.

For the first time, Ansel and his mule worked as a team. Slowly they gained, row by row, making turns with care. They were only a cart-length behind Caballus now, but Ansel had lost count of the rows. He wasn't sure if they were two rows down, or only a few arm spans behind.

Caballus looked over his shoulder and got a shock. He strained harder against his harness, his hooves clawing to find more speed. Ansel realized that from the centaur's greater height, Caballus could clearly see where he and Stump were on the field. He wouldn't be struggling so if he had a two row lead. Ansel smiled viciously and snapped the reigns again.

Legs blurred and hooves pounded the earth like thunder. Caballus's chest flowed with gleaming sweat, and his fur darkened with moisture. Ansel's thighs and calves felt like molten lead pumped through his bloodways, but he would not let up. He was driven like never before, feverish with determination and victory lust.

"YAH!" It was less a command word than a guttural scream from the deep times. It was enough to momentarily silence the crowd, who could scarcely believe that the sound had emerged from one as young as Ansel. Everyone except Yorick, who jumped up and down while pumping his fists in the air.

The last turn complete, Ansel and Caballus started down the final row neck and neck. They were in the center of the field now, just an armspan apart. Caballus pulled down one huge breath after another, trying desperately to feed his enormous lungs. Stump's nostrils flared like cartwheels as he kept up the torturous pace. Ansel spurned him onwards like a man possessed, which wasn't far from reality.

The two competitors threw up enough dust that it became a nearly impenetrable fog. A meek-looking contest official, standing astride the finish line, was the only observer positioned to see the true outcome. With the mule and centaur barreling down upon him, he looked as though he might bolt for safety at any moment.

Somehow, in open defiance of his own good sense and thousands of years of survival instincts, the official managed to keep his feet planted as the two agricultural warriors blew past him in a torrent of horseshoes and flying dirt.

Neither contestant had a clear idea of who had won; the finish had been far too close. His face streaked with upturned earth and his eyes watering from dust, Ansel looked back to the finish line for a decision.

Steadying his frayed nerves with a shot from a concealed hip-flask, the official braced himself and extended a flag to his right; Ansel's side of the field.

He wanted to throw his hands in the air and scream with joy, but Stump was still moving with a purpose. He hadn't been told to stop. "Whoa, Stump!" Ansel pulled back on the reigns until the mule slowed to a walk, then a full, exhausted stop. Ansel was about to tie him off to a post, but Stump lay down with a finality that said he wasn't going anywhere soon.

The static shock of victory still tore through Ansel's body as he jogged over to the stands, preening before the erupting crowd. Some booed and threw heads of lettuce, but most cheered. Everyone loves an underdog.

In the dust cloud behind them, Caballus stood in stunned silence. It took several long moments for his wit to return, but once it did he trotted over to the stands with purpose. The roar of the spectators died down quickly as the centaur approached the new champion from behind.

A chill ran the length of Ansel's spine and then doubled back just to be sure its point had been made. The bravado he'd found after winning the race shrank at the sound of the approaching hooves. He turned around, cautiously, prepared to be trampled by a monster in a berserk fury.

Looming over Ansel nearly a full armspan, Caballus looked upon him with a face of stone. The stands were dead silent. Even the crickets in the grass knew enough to keep quiet. His front legs knelt down, and the horse-man reached out with a meaty, calloused hand and grabbed Ansel's forearm. Someone gasped. Turned out it was Ansel.

But instead of removing the arm from its socket, Caballus hefted it high into the air in honor of the victory, nearly pulling the youth off his feet in the process. The crowd went wild with excitement.

Caballus knelt lower, until his mouth was close enough to Ansel's ear to be heard over the noise. "Your ploughshare, there's something special about it, isn't there?"

Ansel answered him honestly. "I'm not sure, but I think so."

"Where did you get it?"

"My middle brother's blacksmith shop, in Central City."

"I will have to speak with this brother of yours. A blade as fine as that deserves a grander purpose than to toil as a lowly ploughshare, don't you think?"

Ansel nodded blankly. "You're not mad, then?"

"Mad? Of course not, my boy. You won, fair and square. I've had a good run. Besides, I doubt anyone will be challenging me in the Ale Drinking contest for some time, so I'll still have my claim to fame around these parts."

"I suppose so."

"C'mon, lad. Your mule needs water, and you need to rest up for the next heat."

Ansel's face twisted with confusion. "The next heat? But, I beat you already."

"That was just the first round, Son! You still have to face everyone else. But don't worry; the hardest work is already behind you."

The results continued to roll in throughout the afternoon. As the dust cleared after each match, the field judges emerged to score the furrows, but their work was merely a formality at this point. After knocking Caballus out in the first round, the young Deepspade's string of victories each seemed foregone conclusions.

Unalo had remained to watch the boy's assault on the field long after he had expected to be back in his office. Something about the boy scratched at his thoughts and demanded attention.

"And you say you found this boy just last week?"

Mister Vitolo nodded. "Yes, My Lord, out tilling a field as I rode by."

"And he's never competed before?"

"No, My Lord. He's barely spent a day beyond his family's farm."

Unalo scratched an ear while considering this. "How remarkable. What are the other plow-drivers saying? Do they suspect he's cheating in some way?"

Vitolo shook his head. "Not that I've heard. Besides, there's really no good way to cheat at plowing, unless you knick a tendon on someone's animal. And I'm sure Caballus would have said something if it'd happened to him."

"That much is certain." Unalo leaned back into the cushions of his throne. For reasons not immediately apparent, the Deepspade boy had grabbed his interest. His was an old story; a man of meager means achieving fame through talent, hard work, and bravery. It was a compelling story; one that Unalo knew was pure fiction. This Ansel was an ambitious one, and would bear attention. He wanted to get a closer measure of the boy. The duke resolved to stay for the awards ceremony and, provided Deepspade did become champion, hand the trophy to the boy himself.

As it had since translating the scroll, Unalo's mind wandered back to the prophecy. He'd retained Grabber's services, at considerable costs, with open instructions to find and acquire the artifact it spoke of. The text hinted at a weapon, but prophecies weren't famous for precision of language. This meant nearly any object had the potential to be the artifact he sought.

It could prove to be a very long search indeed.

7

The wheat had grown tall and turned to gold. It had been some months since Ansel's stunning upset at the Solstice Festival, and the elation that followed had eroded under the constant labor of his chores. Being the plowing champion had not paid off in a way he had hoped for either.

However, he'd made new and powerful friends. The new duke had congratulated him personally. It was the only time during the whole festival he had done so to any competitor. Perhaps even more unexpected was Caballus himself. Despite his reputation, the centaur had turned out to be a most gracious loser. Even Yorick's hardened opinion of him had been blunted.

Ansel had heeded Caballus's advice. Once the season's plowing was done, he'd taken his impossibly sharp plowshare and converted it into a scythe. The curve of the blade swept the wrong direction for a traditional scythe, but it worked regardless.

He'd toyed with the idea of turning it into a sword, but his father had quashed the notion. *What does a farm kid need a sword for?* Ansel had failed to come up with a convincing answer. It was still a farm tool this way, but at least it wasn't being dragged through the dirt.

He swung it through long arcs as its glimmering edge felled wheat stalks like strands of silk. The heft of the blade and its long shaft had built Ansel's chest and shoulders up rapidly. He was beginning to share Tiklan's silhouette.

As the wheat fell, Elanir followed behind to tie it off into bushels. Her little hands worked the strings into knots with impressive speed. Like everything in her life, she made it into a game; if she could tie them off faster than Ansel could slice, she was winning. Last season, she'd won a lot. This season, however, his new scythe was leaving her in its wake, putting her off her mood.

"Slow down, cheater!"

"How am I cheating?"

"You're bigger than last year!"

"So are you."

"Am not."

Ansel snorted. "Really? The marks on the doorpost tell a different story." But he obliged her anyway and slowed his rate. There was no point finishing before her. He'd just have to turn around and finish whatever bundling she hadn't gotten to yet.

The leisurely pace of the rest of the afternoon suited him just fine. He and Elanir were alone on the farmstead, save for Stump of course. Their father was in town haggling with wheat traders over prices for their harvest. In years past, this would have been done only once the harvest was actually delivered, but lately some idiot had the bright idea to trade in something called wheat 'futures', which Yorick had described as guessing next year's chicken population on last year's eggs.

Ansel didn't understand it, beyond the fact it gave him two unsupervised days to relax just a tad, so maybe it wasn't such an idiotic idea after all. The pair of them worked until midday to clear the back field, took a break for lunch, then resumed clearing the larger north field.

Their pace was leisurely. Elanir's banter had become almost tolerable by mid-afternoon, and Ansel found himself nearly enjoying her company. The only one who wasn't relaxing was Stump. He'd started baying in his stall not long after lunch, and seemed to grow more agitated by the minute.

"Itty, go check on Stump, please. Something's up with him."

"You just want to get ahead of me."

Ansel rolled his head to the sky. "Just go, Itty."

"Don't call me Itty!" she shouted back as she started for the stable. Ansel set the scythe's handle into the ground and leaned on it like a walking stick. The remaining wheat would take the rest of the day to clear, and his shoulders were already beginning to complain from the day's labor. However, Yorick would be back tomorrow and…

Eeeeaak!

The scream came from the direction of the stable. It was unmistakably Elanir's. Ansel grabbed the scythe in one hand and set off at a dead run. One of his sandals broke, so he kicked them off, not caring what the sharp wheat stalks did to the soles of his feet. He could hear Stump's whine join with Elanir's panicked shouts.

It was a wolf pack, had to be. Stump would studiously ignore any lesser predators, or even a lone wolf. Only in numbers were they a danger to the ornery mule. But even a coyote could threaten Elanir, provided it was hungry and desperate enough. With Stump tied up, Ansel was her only defender.

The scythe seemed to grow unbalanced, as though the blade was trying to tip forward. Its edge gleamed so brightly, Ansel thought it was producing light of its own. Then it leapt forward in his hand towards the sounds of trouble, nearly pulling Ansel off his feet. He stumbled, but regained his footing in time, then plunged forward to the stable.

It wasn't wolves, or even coyotes. Surrounding Elanir like a ring of gaunt, feral children were a dozen creatures. They stood on two legs like men, but their bodies were skinny and covered in gray-green skin. Their heads looked too big for their necks, and every part of them seemingly ended with a sharp point.

Goblins.

Ansel had never seen one in person, but like every child, he had heard the stories. Parents in the country told them in hushed whispers just before bedtime, preferably while the wind howled through the cracks to add to the effect. Goblins were terrible creatures; mindless killers who ate the meat of anything they could subdue, even resorting to cannibalism if the situation was dire enough.

But their favorite meal was the tender flesh of naughty children, and they were encircling his sister. The blade of the scythe started to vibrate and glow, but Ansel didn't notice. His eyes were firmly fixed on the closest goblin. The tiny monster's back was turned to him, keeping him ignorant of Ansel's approach.

That oversight cost the goblin its life. Ansel raised the scythe far over his head, reaching for the sun itself, and then brought the blade sweeping down like a tidal wave. The edge rang out a pure tone as it sliced through the creature's knees as easily as the morning's wheat stalks.

Ansel ignored the doomed creature writhing on the ground and shifted his attention to the rest of the raiders, who focused on the new threat in turn.

"Run Itty!" he commanded. But she was too shocked to respond. Her eyes starred vacantly at the legless goblin bleeding to death on the ground. Ansel jumped through the gap in the circle left by the first casualty and stood at its center, brandishing the scythe and daring anyone to be the first to approach.

He didn't have long to wait. Two of them lunged at him from behind, but Ansel heard them and swung about. In a fortuitous accident, the end of the scythe handle caught the nearest one squarely on the side of the head, sending his unconscious body sprawling across the dirt. At the sight of this, the second goblin hesitated for the barest moment, but it was enough. Ansel took advantage of the attacker's uncertainty and completed his sweep, connecting the blade to his neck and following through the chest, finally exiting from under the creature's armpit.

Elanir had collected enough of her wits to make a break for the shelter of the stable through the hole left by the two attackers Ansel had just dispatched. Once there, she did something clever.

She untied Stump.

Unfazed by their dismembered comrades, three more goblins ran up to swarm Ansel. He managed to relieve one of them of its right foot just above the ankle, but the other two closed the gap with unnerving speed. The scythe was never intended to be a weapon of war. It was unwieldy and unbalanced. Its only advantage was the reach it afforded the wielder, but once an enemy was inside that distance, it became worse than useless.

One of the creatures managed to flank him and slashed viciously at his ankle, trying to sever the tendon and immobilize him. It was said goblins preferred their meals still living. But the slice was shallow and Ansel's trousers absorbed much of it. He kicked the attacker in the mouth, stunning it for a moment.

The other goblin lunged forward and sunk dozens of needle-thin teeth into Ansel's forearm. He shrieked in berserk furry, but the goblin only clamped down harder. Ansel's hand opened reflexively and the scythe dropped to the ground.

The rest of the surviving goblins saw the opportunity and pounced. Ansel was overwhelmed by the small, yet surprisingly strong bodies as they pulled him to the ground. The surge of rage and confidence he'd felt at the beginning of the battle had fled the moment he dropped the scythe, replaced now by a rising panic verging on delirium.

A shadow fell over him. He looked up into the smirking face of a goblin, its claws moving into positions over Ansel's eyes. He shrieked with terror and shut his eyes as tight as they would go, but the bone-chilling sound of a goblin's laugh filled the air.

This sound was immediately followed by another; namely the wet cracking sound of a melon being thrown against a rock with some urgency. The shadow disappeared, and the tiny clawed hands holding him down released in a hurry. Confused, Ansel opened his eyes and shot back to his feet.

What he witnessed gave him relief, but did little to alleviate his confusion. The goblins were scattering under the assault of one very irate mule. Now, it should be noted that the natural reaction of most any horse, donkey, or mule was to run from danger. It was apparent, however, that Stump came from a more progressive school of equine thought. The goblin that had been leaning over Ansel lay motionless some distance away, the side of its head reshaped into a soup bowl.

Stump's enormous hind legs lashed out and connected with another unfortunate creature, sending it spinning through the air like a doll thrown in a tantrum. Ansel reached down to recovered his weapon, and immediately felt his confidence and power return.

The remaining goblins fell into disarray. One thought better of it and broke for the crop-line. The rest followed suit in short order. Ansel took a step after them, but remembered Elanir and turned for the stable. She wasn't in sight.

"Itty!" He searched frantically. "Itty, they're gone. You can come out, it's safe."

"Stop calling me Itty," replied a pile of straw. Ansel dropped the scythe and dug through the hay until a small, brunette head popped out. "Elanir, thank the Gods!"

He pulled her out of the pile and dusted her off, checking for injuries as he went. "Are you all right, did they hurt you?" She shook her head, but Ansel could tell she was barely holding back tears.

Much to his relief, she was unhurt, but it was confusing. The goblins had plenty of time to nab her before he got there. Why didn't they? If they weren't after fresh meat, what was the raid for? There hadn't been any talk of goblin raids since before Ansel's brothers had been born. It had been long enough that he'd half expected they were just myths used to scare unruly children. So why did they suddenly reappear now?

He started sweeping around looking for clues. There were tracks everywhere, but they fell into parallel lines near the grain stores behind the stable. Ansel's heart sank as he stepped up the small foot stool to peer inside the huge drums. Their starter seed bin was almost entirely empty. The goblins had stolen the seeds for next season's crops.

His blood boiled at the shear cruelty of it. Carnivores had no use of grain; the monsters took the seed just to steal his family's future. Ansel held the scythe in a death-grip, and his bones cried out for justice. The gleam of the blade transfixed him. It couldn't wait; he would deliver righteous vengeance to the goblin scourge himself.

Ansel stormed back into the stable and grabbed a bridal. Elanir was still sitting on the floor in a haze. A little shudder went through her body when Ansel grabbed her shoulder.

"Elanir, I want you to go in the house and bolt the doors. Wait there until father comes home. Do not come out for any reason. Do you understand?"

She looked at him. Behind her moist eyes, confusion threatened to give way to panic. "But where will you be?"

His face hardened. "I'm going to teach them a lesson."

"By yourself? You'll get hurt, Ansel, you're not a warrior."

Ansel pointed the tip of the scythe at one of the fresh corpses. "Tell that to him. Now, do as I say."

A flicker of opposition ran across her face, but it didn't last. She ran for the house. Ansel heard the bolts slide shut as he mounted Stump and rode away.

An earthworm could follow this trail, Ansel thought. The goblins carried their wounded, making their retreat awkward. Making things even easier was a clear blood trail, likely from the attacker with the missing foot. Still, their speed overland was impressive. He'd been following their tracks for hours, yet still didn't think he'd gained on them appreciably.

The sun hung low in the sky, they would have to stop soon and camp. His quarry, meantime, would likely press on through the night. Ansel spurned Stump forward. Ahead of them loomed the tall, smothering pine trees of the Vinterlong Forest.

Over the centuries, much of the old growth forests of the area had been cleared to make way for fields and pastures. The Vinterlong had… resisted. Its ancient, densely-packed trees were notoriously difficult to cut due to their size alone. However, it was the frequency of accidents that gave the forest its reputation. Dead branches picked the most opportune times to fall from the canopy. Trees that did get cut had a strange habit of twisting around to fall on their assailants. As a species, woodsmen were at least as superstitious as sailors, and most avoided the forest like a crate full of broken mirrors.

As he crossed the line into the forest, Ansel hoped silently that the trees knew the difference between an axe and a scythe. The light faded quickly under the thick canopy, and the air took on a slight chill. The air smelled like musk and gin. Pine needles crunched under Stump's hooves. If the mule was nervous, it didn't show.

"Lucky you," Ansel whispered. There was bit of good news. Between the needles and the strangled light, the forest floor was almost devoid of undergrowth. The trail was even easier to follow in here.

They pressed forward amid the mournful songs of lakir birds. Ansel briefly wondered how they managed to reproduce at all, considering how depressing their mating calls were. It wasn't long before the light disappeared entirely. He knew there was a full moon in the sky somewhere, but the canopy hid all but a few silver strands of moonlight.

It was impossible to continue. Ansel dismounted and fumbled around for a tree to tie Stump off to. For the hundredth time since leaving the farm in a fury, he wished he'd taken a moment to grab a trail pack, a blanket, or even a flint kit. It was going to be a long, probably sleepless night.

He formed a little pile of needles into a pillow and lay down. He crossed the scythe over his chest and shut his eyes out of misplaced optimism. The lakir birds sang him a discomforting lullaby.

Ansel blinked and it was morning. He blinked a few more times to clear his eyes. Little shafts of daylight glowed through the canopy like a candle viewed through burlap. The lakir birds' shift had ended. They'd been replaced by cycads and little chirping birds he didn't recognize.

He sat up, slowly. His stomach roared in protest to the depleted state of its contents. Several varieties of mushroom grew up through the needle bed and on the bark of nearby trees, but he wasn't familiar with them. There were few faster ways to get yourself in trouble in the wild than a sampler platter of unidentified fungus.

With a sickening suddenness, Ansel realized food was not the only thing missing from the area. The tree that should have held Stump's reins was bare. The mule was nowhere to be seen. Even his just-south-of-offensive smell had dissipated.

His stomach stopped grumbling from being empty and started doing backflips from being nervous. He jumped up and ran over to the tree. There was a thin ring of stripped bark from where the leather reins had rubbed at the trunk.

Stump must have worked the knot loose again. Hoof prints led back out of the forest and towards home.

Feeling exposed, Ansel jogged back to his makeshift bed and snatched up the scythe. Tree branches leaned ominously closer, and the sounds of the forest grew dark. Ansel stood at the center of it all defiantly. Once again armed with his special blade, he felt his resolve harden. The blood trail from the previous night had dried, but it was still easy to track.

Now utterly alone, sweat beaded on Ansel's forehead. He faced a stark choice; take the easy, possibly sane path and follow Stump back out of the forest, or continue his one-man crusade against the monsters of his childhood, provided the forest didn't kill him first.

He gently swung the scythe from one trail to the other while he pondered. Oddly, after a few repetitions of this, his arm felt tugged deeper into the woods. Swinging towards the exit was met with resistance, like pushing an oar against the current. He set the implement down on the ground, and watched with growing concern as it twisted towards the blood trail of its own volition.

"What *are* you?" He waited a beat for a response, to no avail.

"Great," he sighed heavily. "I'm alone in a cursed forest, trailing monsters, with only a possessed farm tool for company." He plucked up the scythe again and spent a few moments trying to reconstruct the decision tree that had led him here, in the hope that he might live long enough to learn from his mistakes.

The scythe continued to tugging away like an eager puppy. He had to admit, it felt good in his hand. He felt three arm spans tall whenever he held it. It hadn't let him down yet; at the plowing competition, on the battlefield, it had held up its end of the deal.

Maybe it was trying to tell him something. Maybe the blade was setting him on a path, and whatever happened to him would happen to it, right? It wouldn't endanger itself just to send him to his doom; that would be ridiculous.

His heart swelled with confidence. Now certain of the correct course, Ansel spun about on his heel and took up the blood-trail once more in pursuit of his quarry.

He made it three steps before the snare tripped and yanked him high into the air by his ankle.

"He did what?!"

Elanir withered under her father's anger. Intellectually, she knew it wasn't directed at her, but she'd never before heard Yorick shout. He never had to; he was more than intimidating enough at a simple conversational level.

"He left with Stump to try and get our seeds back from the goblins."

"I can buy more seeds! What was that idiot thinking?"

"I don't know, Daddy. I tried to stop him, but he wasn't himself."

Yorick paced the floor of the farmhouse. "He was blood-drunk. I've seen it before."

"Where?"

"Nevermind, where, Elanir. I'm taking you down the road to stay with the Porters until I get back."

"Where are you going?"

"After your brother, of course. I'll need to get some men from town and…"

As he spoke, a familiar whiny sent Yorick running for the window.

"It's Stump. Gods, he's out of time. Elanir, grab a couple dresses and a blanket, then get outside now!"

Elanir obeyed, then spent the rest of the morning trying to stay out of the way of the brewing storm that was her father.

Blood rushed to Ansel's head as he swung from the rope, muddling his thinking. His left foot had been taken in the snare and fell asleep almost immediately. He swung from a thick pine bough at least six arm spans in the air. Even if he could cut the rope, the bed of needles wouldn't be nearly enough cushion to break his fall without injury.

It was a moot point anyway; he'd dropped the scythe at the sudden jerk of the rope. Now it lay directly below him, tauntingly in sight, yet totally out of reach. Then an even more distressing realization struck him. The birds were as silent as temple mice. It felt as though the entire forest held its breath in anticipation of what happened next.

Through eyes blurred by the blood pooling in his head, Ansel made out movement in the spaces between trees trunks. Peering down as he was, all he could see were the tops of their heads, but it was enough to identify them as some of the same goblins from the raid. Several new additions had joined their ranks as well, including a giant among goblins. He stood at least a full head above the rest. He was only a fraction shorter than Ansel himself. The giant goblin strode into the clearing and stood directly under the spot where Ansel swung in the breeze.

Ansel had to crane his neck back painfully to keep the goblin in sight. The creature reached out a foot to the scythe's handle and flicked it away with a contemptuous little kick. Then he turned his slit-pupil eyes up to meet Ansel's and spoke.

"You in a cucumber, I think." He smiled revealed a hundred or more pinprick teeth. Ansel's forearm throbbed from where one of the goblins had bitten him yesterday. But it was the odd vegetable reference that stuck in his head.

"Ah, do you mean a pickle, maybe?"

"Sorry?"

"Well you said cucumber. We say 'You're in a pickle.'"

The goblin's smile faded into annoyance. "Is my human no good? Maybe we have conversation in my language. That be better?"

"No, no!" Ansel backtracked faster than a golem with its feet on the wrong way around. "You're doing just fine."

The smile returned. "Good. Now, what I do about you? Let you down?"

"Thank you, no. I'm perfectly comfortable right here."

This wasn't the answer the goblin had expected. "Comfortable? You pass out by dark, be dead in a day."

"I'll take that over being eaten,' Ansel said flatly. It wasn't the most diplomatic response.

"You think we hungry?" Ansel nodded. "Then why trap you? Could have cut you neck in sleep." The goblin traced a line across his own throat with a black claw. "Less trouble than a trap."

Ansel had to admit, the goblin had a point. But that just raised another question. "Why did you trap me, then?"

"Want to talk."

"Talk? You could have just woken me up!"

The creature shook his head. "No way. You dangerous."

"Me? I'm just a kid, how am I dangerous?"

With a gesture that crossed the bounds of species, the goblin rolled his eyes like a pair of dice. "You joke with me, yes? You kill four of us, cut off foot of a fifth, just with a wheat-sword, and you ask how you dangerous? No play stupid with me."

"But you were attacking my home. Your... men were going to eat my little sister."

It was clear by now that the speaker was the group's leader. The rest of the goblins were doing their best to avoid looking straight at him. Maybe he was even their king. The leader looked down and spoke to one of his men in a chittering tongue that sounded like huge crickets.

He tilted his head back up to regard Ansel once more. "We did not eat you broodmate, did we?"

"Well, no, but your men surrounded her and she was terrified. Everyone knows goblins steal children and eat them."

"Do they now? Did we take your broodmate?" Ansel was forced to shake his head. "We take seed, not chill-der-an, yes?" Ansel nodded. "Why you think?"

"I don't know. To starve us out? That was our starter seed for next season."

The leader looked through him for a long moment, like he was trying to work out a vexing math problem. Finally, he gave a nod to one of his men. It took four of them to lower Ansel down without pulling them off their feet, but inch by inch he was returned to the ground.

He sat up to remove the rope from his ankle, but fell right back over from a surge of dizziness. Ansel felt small, sharp hands grabbing at his feet, but he was too disoriented to react with anything more than a half-hearted kick.

"They take off rope. Let them." He leaned over Ansel's head with a predatory, yet inquisitive look. Those goblins not working to free his foot kept a respectful distance. Whether it was from himself or their leader, Ansel couldn't tell. The rope came off and blood rushed back into his left foot. It felt like being stung by an entire nest of frozen wasps.

"It wake up again soon. Then, we walk."

"Walk?" Ansel's alarm rose. "Walk where? Am I your prisoner?"

The leader shook his head. "No. But it time you pink-skins see something, I think."

They marched for the rest of the morning and into the afternoon. Despite their short stature, Ansel found keeping pace with the line of goblins difficult. They seemed to flow over obstacles like water, while every fallen tree trunk slowed him down as he stopped to climb over it.

As the light again began to fade, the leader, who had taken up station at the head of the procession, came to an abrupt stop. Directly ahead of him was a mighty oak tree, overturned by wind which must have been mightier still. Half of its roots were thrust into the air like a giant spider's web.

The king goblin walked to the very center of the web and rapped on the core of the roots not once, but four distinct times. Each series of knocks was met with a corresponding series from the inside.

Apparently satisfied that the person on the outside was who they claimed to be, the roots at the base of the great tree untangled like a bouquet of snakes, revealing a tunnel heading into the earth at a steep angle. A small, light-skinned goblin with sunken eyes stood at attention on the other side with his gaze cast towards the ground.

The lead goblin started down the tunnel, the rest of his troupe close behind. No one prodded or pushed at Ansel to follow, but it was still obvious that he was expected to do so. The already weak light was quickly snuffed out as he moved down the corridor. The air took on an unseasonable chill as well. The darkness slowed him to a snail's pace, forcing him to feel his way down the tunnel by hand and foot.

Gritty topsoil soon gave way to cool, roughly hewn bedrock. Every twenty arm spans or so, the tunnel made a dog-leg turn. Ansel couldn't figure out why at first, until he realized how much easier a kinked tunnel would be to defend from intrusion. Ahead, he saw the warm yellow glow of light start to shine off the moisture slicked walls.

Ansel came around the final dog-leg and the tunnel flared out like the horn of a trumpet. Brilliant light cascaded down from the ceiling, illuminating a huge cavern. It was massive, large enough to house an entire village, and even a lake. Some portions of the space looked to be natural cave, while others gave the impression of having been carved out of the rock by hand. On the walls, there were three, even four layers of cubby holes dug out of the rock face.

At first, Ansel had assumed the light came in through skylights carved into the ceiling. But upon closer inspection, he realized that it was actually artificial. Suspended from the roof were dozens, even hundreds of glowing orbs. Judging their size was difficult, as it was hard to tell exactly how tall the cavern was. The scale of it was that disorienting.

The goblin king watched from a short distance away as Ansel took in the scene. His face was impassive as he peered at his guest. The rest of the party from the forest watched him apprehensively. One of them held onto his scythe for safekeeping.

The air carried the same strange chittering voices rising from the village. Slowly, other goblins started to emerge from their huts and hollowed-out stone houses. A crowd formed around the foreigner in their midst. But the curious onlookers were different from the raiders Ansel had fought at the farm. Even for goblins, they were perilously thin, nearly emaciated. They had the same listless, sunken eyes as the door guard. Some of them stared at him with a feral intensity, but most just gazed at him with a sort of forlorn hopelessness. Despite their alien features, Ansel felt his stomach sink in response to their plight.

Ansel looked to the leader. "What happened to them?"

The king turned around and started walking. He looked over his shoulder to Ansel to say only, "Come."

The crowd parted to let them by, as guarded whispers ran through it like leaves rustling in the breeze. He followed the king down through the village. Several other goblins kept pace a few strides behind him. Curious little faces peered out through windows as the procession passed by. They were mostly children, but even they had not been spared whatever had struck their elders.

Something else about the village struck Ansel. There almost seemed to be *two* villages, one overlapping the other. The organically shaped mud-and-post huts, while well-built and quite large, stood in stark contrast with the crisp, squared-off stone homes interspersed throughout the streets. It was as if two entirely different cultures had built on the same grounds without one taking notice of the other.

Ansel was about to ask the leader about this incongruity, but as they crossed a final street and exited the village, the sight beyond stole his breath away. It took him several heartbeats before he found words again.

"They're fields. You have wheat fields underground."

He was exercising his muscles of obviousness, for stretching out many hundreds, perhaps a thousand arm spans, were fields of wheat bathed in light from the glowing spheres above. They were separated into a grid; each square of grain outlined by a channel of water, with gravity feed troughs to irrigate the crops. The channels were fed in turn by a waterway dug from the lake on the other side of the village, with locks and small dams to control its flow.

It was an awe-inspiring scene. And it answered many questions. Chief among them was why the goblin raids had come to a halt all those years ago, and why little children had stopped disappearing. The goblins had turned to agriculture. They had civilized themselves.

Still the farmer, Ansel ran down to get a better look at the water system, the soil, and the grain itself. But as he drew closer, it became apparent something was wrong. The smell was the first sign; it was bitter and had a faint whiff of decay. Not at all like healthy wheat. Then, he was close enough to see the wheat stalks, and the rest of the village's sobering story came into focus.

He grabbed a stalk and inspected the leaves. Black spots with a tiny tuff of white fur at the center infested the entire surface. Then he looked to the grain at the very top of the plant. It was entirely dissolved, turned into a pungent, useless black sludge.

"Blighted." Ansel slung the word like a curse. He realized

the goblin king was standing beside him, his angular face trying and failing to conceal his anger and desperation. Still holding the diseased stalk, Ansel looked to the king.

"You're all starving. That's why you took our seeds."

The king nodded. There was one point Ansel still didn't understand about the situation. "But what do you do with the wheat? You're meat-eaters, aren't you?"

The king pointed at a huge hole about midway down the side of the cavern. "Next cave full of sheep, chickens. We grow wheat, feed animals, animals make dirt, feed wheat. We eat animals. All dead now. Make jerky from them, but run out soon."

Ansel beamed up at the goblin. They had built an entire society under the ground, completely self-contained and content to leave the rest of the world alone while they worked to better themselves. And it was all coming apart because of a few spores.

"The seeds your men took won't help you." He pointed at the ruined grain. "It's a fungus, you see, like tiny mushrooms. The still air and humidity down here probably just make things worse. If you replant, it will just happen again."

"See this before?"

"The blight? I haven't, no. But my father did, before I was born. It was terrible. Three straight seasons of failed crops. Hundreds starved, hundreds more moved away and never came back."

"How do you beat it?"

"Eventually the..." Ansel's mind stopped dead. With the blights of a generation ago, new strains of wheat arose that resisted the fungus. They only yielded two thirds the grain per field as the regular strains, but they grew healthy. Once the blight had been eradicated, farms returned to the original, higher-yielding strains. But it was whispered that a supply of the resistant seeds were maintained in the castle, as insurance against the blight's return.

Gears slipped back into place, and Ansel continued. "If

I can help save your village, will you let me go free and promise to stop the raids?"

The king looked surprised and more than a little offended. "Free? You no prisoner. I tell you already."

Ansel put his hands in front of him. "I'm sorry. Will you promise not to send out any more raids, then?"

The goblin crossed his arms. "We only raid because we hungry. Need fresh seed, or we return to being animals."

"Yes, but not just any seed. You need the *right* seed, or it's all for nothing."

"And you have *right* seed?"

"No, but I know where to find it."

The leader eyed him with great suspicion for a long, uncomfortable moment. "Two days ago, you kill four of us. Now you offer help?"

"I didn't understand two days ago. Now I do. I don't want your people going back to the raids and kidnappings and killings. And I believe that you don't want that for your people either."

They stared at each other for a long time. Ansel decided to break the silence. "What's your name?"

The goblin leader's face contorted in surprise and affront. "No give name to stranger. Name has power, can hunt someone with their name. Leave name everywhere like a scent, people find you easy."

Ansel found the idea completely foreign. The first thing two humans did when they met was exchange names. However, that didn't make the goblin's words wrong. Names did indeed hold power, one he'd never contemplated until just now.

A power he decided to use.

He extended a hand. "My name is Ansel Deepspade, and I want to help you."

The discussions went on for hours. The language barrier was a large obstacle to overcome, especially considering that the king was the only goblin who could speak even broken common, and that he seemed to lack any understanding of tense. When who would do what was a frequent point of miscommunication.

Most of the village had turned out to listen to the deliberations. There were no secret meetings among goblins. Eventually, however, the goblin king and the farm-boy reached an accord. Now it was going to be up to him to somehow see it through to the end. By the time they had drank the ceremonial tuber beer to seal the agreement, the king carried himself with guarded optimism. They even returned Ansel's scythe as a sign of respect. It was a largely symbolic gesture; he was outnumbered by the hundreds.

The king led the procession back up the tunnel to the world above, with Ansel walking close behind. He still couldn't see much of anything, but he could hear the king's footsteps and simply matched his pace. He held the long handle of the scythe ahead of him as an alarm for the dog-legs in the tunnel.

A commotion came from ahead. The king stopped as frantic footsteps ran down the tunnel from the portal. Ansel could only make out silhouettes, and couldn't understand any of the words, but he'd heard enough of the goblin's language to detect the alarm in the door guard's strained voice.

The king listened intently until his guard had finished. He asked a couple of brief questions, then turned around and faced Ansel. Just the barest glint of light shined back through the goblin's pupils.

"Humans at the door. You send for help?"

"No! I came alone, you know that. I've been with you this whole time, how could I send for..."

Twilight eyes peered at him intently. "Speak."

"Is there a mule with them, a gray mule with a black mane?"

"What is 'mule'?"

"Like a horse, except longer ears and square face."

The king turned back to the guard and shared a curt exchange. "Yes, there is mule."

"That's Stump. I rode him into the forest. He escaped last night and probably went straight home. My father's out there. I can talk to them." He didn't wait for permission. Instead, he pushed past the king and guard and ran up the last leg of the tunnel. The air up here was warm again. Little pin-pricks of light shone through tiny gaps between the enmeshed tree roots. He stood there waiting for the roots to part, but nothing happened. He pushed on the web to no avail.

He called back down the tunnel. "Is there a lever or something? I can't get it open."

"Command word," replied the king.

"Well, what is it?"

"No tell you. Keep humans away."

A heavy, chunking sound fell on the other side of the roots. It came again, and again. It fell into a steady beat. Ansel knew it was the sound of an ax. "You can't keep them out. Listen, they are chopping through right now."

The king turned around and barked a set of terse orders.

"What did you just order them to do?"

"Use other exits. Come from many sides. Stop attack."

"No!" Ansel punched at the door. "They're only here because they think I've been kidnapped. If they know I'm okay, this all stops. Let me see them."

In the dim light, Ansel watched the king as he worked through the problem. The thud of the ax punctuated the silence like a musician keeping time.

"Please! Let me end this!"

"You no want you father get hurt, dead."

"I don't want *anyone* getting hurt or dead, on either side.

There's been enough of that already."

"From *you,*" the king added pointedly.

"Yes, a mistake I'm ashamed of. Let me stop them from making it again."

The king glared at him for another heartbeat, but then he leaned forward and spoke something completely unintelligible to the door. Whatever he said did the trick and the roots untangled. The king fell behind Ansel and gave him a rough little shove out the door.

The light change was too abrupt. It took a moment for his eyes to adjust. But once they did, some long-forgotten part of his brain set to work prioritizing the threats it saw. First on the list were the tips of four heavy crossbow bolts. Next, the edge of a huge, double-headed battle ax, most recently employed chopping into the door. Last on the list, yet the most intimidating, was the face of his father, twisted by conflicting emotions of relief and rage until it looked like a crumpled washcloth.

He set down the crossbow and rushed at his son. Ansel went stiff, unsure if he was about to be hugged or whipped. Apparently Yorick's relief won out, because he slid to a stop and embraced his son with arms of solid oak. Tears pooled at the corners of his eyes.

"Ansel, thank the Gods. I thought you were eaten for sure."

"I'm fine." Ansel tried to wriggle free of the iron hug, but failed. "The goblins don't…"

"Yorick," boomed a voice like boulders colliding, "fall back to the line!"

Ansel looked up and realized it was Caballus. The centaur stood behind the other crossbowmen, wearing a chest plate and buckler shield on his right arm, while brandishing a malicious barbed lance in his left. Strapped to the sides of his horse body was a pair of wickedly curved falchions.

Only then did Ansel notice that his father was wearing a fine, chainmesh shirt, studded leather gorget, and brass grieves. They were well-fitted and had the dings and scuffs that promised tales of great battles. Before he could ask his father where they'd come from, he was lifted off his feet as though he weighed no more than a barn cat and carried back behind the line. Yorick set him down and retrieved his crossbow.

"Quickly now, before they close the door."

Ansel's alarm rose. "What are you doing?"

Caballus glanced down at him. "Eradicating this nest. We can't have them coming back."

The boy jumped up and grabbed Caballus's lance with both hands. "No, you don't understand. I wasn't captured…"

Behind him, the roots started to weave themselves closed again. "No time!" his father said. "We have to move."

"Listen to me!" Ansel screamed. "First of all, that's not a nest down there, it's an entire village. There are hundreds of goblins at the end of the tunnel, and they can see in the dark."

This bit of intelligence gave everyone pause. Ansel soldiered on. "And they didn't kidnap me. They don't eat people anymore, they're farmers now."

"Hah!" One of the other farmers snorted. Ansel recognized him as Mister Lorian; he'd plowed his field. "That's a fib, that is. Who ever heard of a farmin' gobber?"

"I have!" Ansel snapped back. "I spent all of the day with them. They grow wheat underground and use it to feed sheep. That's where they get their meat now, and it's why no one's seen them for twenty years."

He finally had their attention, if only due to the abject absurdity of the story he was telling. But, it was enough; the delay allowed the portal to finish closing. He seemed to be the only one to notice.

"But they attacked our farm, Son. Elanir told me everything."

"Including how you ran off to take on the whole brood by yourself," added a smiling Caballus cheerfully.

Yorick's face hardened for a moment as he looked at his son. "We'll discuss that more, later." Ansel's gut bottomed out. He wasn't going to get away from this misadventure scot-free after all. "Now Ansel, if they're peaceful farmers, why did they raid our home?"

"I was coming to that." Ansel's voice held a bit more irritation than he'd intended to let slip, but if Yorick heard it he let it slide. "They didn't come for Itty or me, they came for seeds. At first I thought they were trying to starve us to be cruel, but they needed the seeds because their wheat crop failed."

"Why did it fail?"

"Blight."

Every face in the posse cringed at the word. Many of them were old enough to remember first-hand the last famine. If a vote was taken to see what was more frightening, the return of the goblins or the blight, it would split squarely down the middle.

Yorick kept the probe going. "If that's true, our seed isn't going to do them any good."

"Yes, but they didn't know that," Ansel explained. "They've only been farming for a generation. They've never seen blight before." He took a deep breath, knowing that he was about to step off a very high cliff. "So, we have to go to Duke Gerkolis and convince him to trade them some of the blight seeds."

8

Holeck's head appeared through the door into Unalo's office. "I'm sorry to trouble you, 'Milord, but there is a group of men at the gate asking for an audience."

Unalo looked up from a tax collection report with a quizzical air. "What sort of group?"

"I believe the appropriate term would be a 'rabble', 'Milord."

"Well, then shoo them off."

"They are quite determined, Sire."

Unalo's left eyebrow inched up. "What sort of 'determined'? Pitchfork-and-battering-ram determined, or hunger-strike-at-the-wall determined?"

"More the latter than the former, 'Milord, except these men seem well fed enough."

"Did they say what they wanted?"

"Not beyond speaking to you, Sire."

Unalo stood up from his chair and walked to the room's only window. From this vantage, he could see the castle's gate. The heavy oak doors stood open for the day's trade business, yet the group of peasants stood patiently on the other side; among them was a boy with a familiar face.

"My word, is that the plowing champion with them?"

Holeck peered out the window. "Yes, 'Milord, along with his father. The centaur, Caballus, was with them as well; although I don't see him just now."

"Send them up."

"Sire?"

"Now, if you please."

Holeck cocked an eyebrow, but obeyed and left the office. Unalo smirked. Ansel Deepspade, the unlikely champion. He'd wanted to keep tabs on the ambitious young man. His unexpected reappearance made the task all the easier.

He tidied his desk, tucking the tax report into a drawer, along with several magic scrolls he had rescued from the chaos of the archives for identification. They'd been lost in that mess for years, they could wait another day.

Soon, Holeck reappeared with the duke's guests, and a tray of refreshments. The young man followed his father through the door. Oddly, once inside the room, the six men arranged themselves behind the boy, as though he had been picked as spokesman. Holeck set a cup of tea on his desk.

"Ah, young Deepspade. Please, help yourselves to some tea. What brings our reigning plow champion to my office?"

Ansel seemed hesitant. It took a little nudge from his father, to get him started.

"Good morning, Sir," the boy said meekly.

"It's "Milord, or Sire, if you please."

"Oh. Sorry, Sir, I mean 'Milord."

Unalo gave the youth a disarming smile. "Think nothing of it. What can I do for you?"

"Well, 'Milord, we came to ask you for a supply of blight seeds."

Unalo drew a blank. Agriculture had not been his main area of study during his ascension. He looked to Holeck to fill in the gaps. His chief of staff leaned in and whispered a brief explanation.

"Ah, of course. But to what end? The blight hasn't returned, I trust?"

The boy shook his head. "No, 'Milord, at least not to our lands. Er, your lands."

Unalo made note of the correction. The boy recognized

his authority, at least. "Well that is a relief. Why then do you ask for the seed?"

Ansel visibly paused to compose himself. *Oh, this should be good,* thought Unalo.

"Well, 'Milord, it's like this. We've discovered a goblin village in the Vinterlong Forest. They've learned how to farm and raise animals to eat. That's why there haven't been any raids for so long. But now their wheat crops have caught the blight and they're starving. If we give them the blight seeds, they can take care of themselves again."

Unalo made a show of sinking into his high-backed chair and lacing his fingers, a look of heavy contemplation on his face. He held this pose for several seconds. "What do the goblins have to trade for this service?"

The question startled his guest. "Trade? Nothing, they're starving. They stole our seeds hoping they could start over."

"They've restarted the raids? Now that is disturbing." Unalo rubbed his chin somewhat theatrically.

"They were desperate. They weren't coming for people, just seeds."

"Yes, but you have to look at this from my perspective, my young friend. You are asking me to reward their bad behavior. Once they learn that violence will get them what they want, it will only escalate."

"But it will escalate anyway. Once their meat runs out, they'll have no choice to go back to the way they were before. Their king doesn't want them to go back to being monsters."

"They have a king, do they? And he picked you as an intermediary? Quite impressive, Mister Deepspade, or shall I call you Ambassador Deepspade?" A smile still graced Unalo's face, but it had taken on a more intimidating curl.

"It's not like that, 'Milord," Ansel said quickly. "It's just I'm the only person they know."

"I see. Well, it was good of you to take on the responsibility, regardless. But, I must decline. Handing over the seeds now would send the wrong message to the goblins, as well as our own people."

"But if the goblins starve, they'll go back to raiding for meat, stealing children just like in the stories."

"Perhaps. But if that happens, now we know where their village is, thanks to you. We can attack and end the problem permanently. I'm sure we would have no shortage of volunteers for the militia."

"What do you mean?"

One of his other guests snorted at the question, but Ansel's father shot him a pointed look and he returned to silence. Ansel looked confused.

"What your compatriot was trying to say is simply that, historically, goblins have not been a very popular species. While you may have seen their miraculous transformation, the rest of the population has not. Old prejudices die hard, Mister Deepspade. And many among my people would have serious questions about my rule if one of my first acts was to capitulate to them."

Unalo's voice became conciliatory. "You must understand, I am a duke at the very beginning of his time. My people are looking to my leadership for strength and stability. People need to have confidence in their leaders, or the order of things begins to decay. That's part of why I'm here today and Lord Blyton is not."

"But you have the power to, don't you?"

"In theory, yes. But power is a fickle thing. If I don't consider the needs and opinions of the people, then I am little more than a despot, and they don't have very healthy life expectancies.

"What you ask is too radical. If the goblins can find some way to barter for the seeds, it will be good for both species. It might even start to open trade between us. But if I just *give* them the seeds, I'll look weak to both goblin and man alike. I can't afford that."

"But..." Ansel began. However, his father interrupted him with a thick hand placed gently on his shoulder.

"That's enough, Son. You made your case. It's the duke's decision to make."

Unalo nodded to him. "A difficult one, I would add. But, enough of business. So, young Deepspade, will we see you and your amazing plow return to the festival next season to defend your title?"

Ansel shrugged his shoulders. "Maybe, but I'd already converted the ploughshare into a scythe for the wheat harvest. I don't know if I'm going to switch it back or just buy a new one."

"Well perhaps you can enter the fall reaping tournament, then. I look forward to watching you compete again, regardless. It was most invigorating last time."

"Thank you, 'Milord," the youth said uncertainly.

"Now, if you'll excuse me, I have more business to attend. The only thing that grows faster than the wheat around here seems to be the stacks of petitions."

"Yes, 'Milord, of course," said the boy's father as he spun his son around towards the door. "Thank you for being so generous with your time."

"Think nothing of it, Mister Deepspade. Good day."

After the rabble had filed back out of his office, Unalo called Holeck back over. "Is Grabber still in the castle, or has he left again?"

Holeck shrugged." Who knows? He's slippery as a frog; even I can't keep track of his comings and goings."

"See if you can round him up, will you?"

"Yes, 'Milord."

Barely enough time had passed for Unalo to finish his tea when someone wrapped at the door. A thin, dagger-shaped ear slid through. "You summoned me?"

"Yes, come in."

The goblin thief sat down in the far chair, always just at the edge of vision.

"I must say, I'd half expected you to sneak out of the shadows the moment I asked for you."

Grabber smiled. "Even a goblin has to eat."

"Interesting that you should say so."

Grabber cocked a thin eyebrow. "Yes?"

"Apparently, a rather progressive colony of your people in the Vinterlong is experiencing a famine. Do you know anything about it?"

The goblin made a small chucking noise that Unalo had come to recognize as dismissal.

"I have a contact in that village. Their king's a loon. Twenty odd years ago, the last king of that clan led a raid on a dwarf cave…"

"There are dwarves living in the Vinterlong?" Unalo interrupted.

"All sorts of things live in the Vinterlong. Anyway, the raid was a smashing success and they took over the whole settlement. Except the king was killed in battle. So his son took over and got this crazy idea to keep the dwarves' agriculture going."

"Why?"

"He wanted to 'civilize' his clan. Stop the raids that killed his father. Like putting a coronation gown on a dog, if you ask me."

"That's an unexpected observation, coming from a civilized goblin."

"I ain't civilized," Grabber snapped. "I'm a thief and killer. Just because I can talk and read doesn't make me civilized. I'm not trying to deny my nature, only perfect it."

Unalo turned his palms upwards. "My mistake, sorry if I've offended you. Have you heard anything about the famine in this mad king's village?"

"Yes, the wheat crop failed to some disease. They sent out a party to some local farm to steal seed to try and restart, but the raid went sour."

"What happened?"

"The party was slaughtered. The survivors said some farm kid was possessed by Chun himself and tore through them all by himself with nothing but a wheat scythe."

Unalo froze at the mention of the scythe. Then, his mind took a turn and started running. "This boy, what happened to him? Was he killed?"

"No, the raiders ran from the carnage. Apparently, the little idiot chased after them all by himself."

"Some might call that bravery," Unalo interjected.

"Can't collect the medals when you're dead. Anyway, they captured him, but the king took pity and spared him."

"How long ago did this happen?"

"Just recently, maybe two days."

It fits, Unalo thought, *it all fits. He wins the plow competition against all expectation, then makes a scythe out of it and miraculously survives not one, but two encounters with goblins.*

"Grabber, have you made any headway finding that special artifact we've discussed?"

"To be blunt, no. You haven't given me much to work with, and there are a lot of 'special artifacts' floating around since all the looting in Central City last year. It's hard to know where to start."

The duke smirked coolly. "I think I can narrow it down."

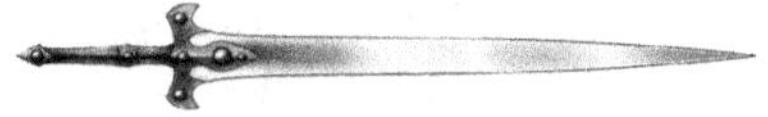

The moon above was barely a sliver as Grabber made his way across the wheat field. The field provided far less cover for his approach than it would if the crop hadn't been harvested. No matter, the dark of night was insurance enough against prying human eyes. The only light came from the stars above and the short green bursts of those cursed flameflies.

The farmstead was directly ahead, but his objective was almost certainly in one of the out buildings. But which one? This was the problem with residential jobs. Finding valuables in castles, temples, and mansions was easy; just find the most heavily-defended, inaccessible room on the property and from there, lock picks, bribe money, and the occasional stone-molding scroll were all that was needed for most jobs.

But civilians, they were intolerable. Half the time, they were too ignorant to know the true value of their possessions. You were likely as not to find a priceless urn out in the garden with petunias growing from it as hidden properly. Objectives could be anywhere.

Hidden in plain sight, thought the goblin. Just as the scroll had said. He picked a shed at random and swept in, gently as a breeze. Even in the near dark, his trained eyes quickly inventoried the building's contents. Farm implements were hardly his forte, but it didn't need to be. Instead of trying to identify every bizarre object, he simply sorted them into 'scythe' and 'not a scythe'. This shortcut sped things up considerably.

The first shack a bust, he slinked on to the next one. In the category of 'not a scythe', there was an ornery-looking mule. It eyed him with a level of malice not usually present in herbivores. Grabber gave the animal a wide berth as he scanned the stable. No luck. The last shed was just a lean-to. It held nothing more than seed and grain bins. He climbed up the small steps and ran an arm through the grain in case anything was hidden within. Nothing.

This left just the farmhouse itself, and presumably the owners of the farm were asleep in their beds. There were five points of entry; two doors and three windows. The doors were shut, and had rusty, hand-beaten iron hinges. They would squeak loud enough to wake the oak trees on the other side of the field if opened.

That left the windows. Grabber surveyed each in turn and settled on the one looking into the kitchen. There was no glass, so he slipped inside without a sound. It was even darker inside the farmhouse. There were no candles or rolling fires in the hearth. It was not as quiet, fortunately. In the next room, a man snored loudly enough that it could be felt through the floorboards. That would make things easier.

Unsurprisingly, the scythe wasn't in the kitchen. There was a trap door built into the floorboards, probably a root cellar. He opened it with the pull rope and peered into the small cavern. The smell of mildew wafted up from the cellar. Potatoes, yams, sugar beets, not much else.

Only the bedroom remained. The goblin slid into the room without trouble. It would have been nearly impossible to make enough noise to be heard above the snoring, even if he'd tried. The family all slept in the same room. The father was the source of the cataclysmic noise and slept alone on the left side of a bed big enough for two. The son and daughter slept against the wall in two beds stacked one atop the other.

Leaning against the wooden frame of their beds, was his objective. The scythe's reverse-swept blade gleamed even in the near-dark of the room. Grabber had the disconcerting feeling that the blade was smiling at him, the sort of smile meant only to reveal the size and number of one's teeth.

He shook off the thought and approached. The scythe's wooden handle was strangely curved and nearly twice as tall as Grabber himself. Carrying it would be awkward. For a moment, he considered removing the blade and leaving the handle behind. Surely any enchantments would be in the metal. A quick glance up to the blade dispelled that idea. The keened edge peered down at him like an eager guillotine. He'd keep the handle in place; anything that kept that blade as far away as possible was welcome.

For all their stealth and agility, goblins weren't very strong. Grabber favored daggers, crossbows, and poisons over axes, bows, and long swords. So it should have come as no surprise that when he tried to heft the ungainly scythe, it twisted in his hands. The blade struck the wood bed-frame and rang out in a crystal-clear 'E' sharp, loud enough to nearly match the rhythmic rumbling coming from the other side of the room.

Grabber froze while the resonant blade sang out for help.

An eternity later, it finally died down, subsumed by the father's snoring. The goblin let out a relieved sigh.

"You shouldn't be here."

Grabber actually jumped. It had been years since that happened. He didn't *get* startled, he was just a carrier. He looked for the voice and found himself staring into the hardened face of a small human girl. She sat up on the bottom bed with a look of grating overconfidence that only the truly naïve can produce.

His right arm moved in a blur and Grabber pulled a poison-slicked dagger from somewhere in the folds of his tunic. "Make another sound, whelp, and you're dead."

Infuriatingly, she just smirked. "Make one twitch and I'll scream, then my brother or daddy will pop your little green head off like a dandelion."

Who does this broodling think she's talking to? Grabber thought. She was just a child, but her tiny, arrogant voice cut under his skin. His left hand dropped from the scythe and lashed out to grab her by the mouth. He let the tips of his claws sink into her cheeks a tiny fraction, just enough to create five little rivets of crimson. Her mask of confidence evaporated as his palm muffled the sudden shriek.

The goblin held the stiletto lightly but firmly against the bloodway in the girl's neck. "Shut up," he instructed coolly. Her struggles ceased, and he was rewarded with silence.

Silence. Something important was missing. An alarm went off in his mind, but it was a beat too late. Grabber looked to the other side of the room, where the snoring of a cave troll *should* have been coming from, only to see the father sitting bolt upright, fully awake, and reaching for a taut, loaded crossbow.

"Lay a finger on that bow and she dies from Adorian scorpion venom. Slow and painful."

"Won't do you any good, goblin. You'll be staked to the wall behind you either way." In the low light, the man's face looked like a statue; hard and implacable, no emotion except focus. It was not the face of a simple farmer.

"What's going on, Father?" The new voice came from the bed above Grabber's head. He glanced up for just a moment to see a boy's worried face staring down at him. The father took advantage of the lapse and lunged for the crossbow, getting a hand on the stock.

Grabber tensed up his arm and pressed the dagger ever so slightly into the girl's neck. "That's enough!" he barked. "So much as a blink and she dies."

His face still a mask of marble, the man's hand slowly retreated from the crossbow. "Ansel, let it go."

The bedframe above him creaked. Grabber looked up just in time to see the boy's hand withdrawing from the scythe's shaft, which was precisely the moment that his hostage chose to bite his hand.

He shouted a curse in the old tongue and grabbed her forehead instead. The girl spat a mouthful of his dark blood onto the floor.

"Shoot him, Daddy!" she yelled.

"Elanir," the father said calmly, "don't struggle. Do as the goblin says for now."

Grabber's mind spun. What *was* it with these people? He was supposed to be stealing a farm tool from peasants. It should have been easier than taking lakir eggs from their ground nests. But these people, they were cold and fearless. He'd stolen from princes, even kings who didn't show this level of resolve and composure. He suddenly wanted to be as far away from this house as possible.

"Good. Now, I am leaving. Give chase and she dies."

"What assurance do I have that you will release her?"

The possibility of swapping the girl for the scythe occurred to him, but once he released her, there was no way Grabber would be able to outrun that damned crossbow bolt.

"None, because I won't. You'll be contacted with terms of an exchange within three days."

"No deal." It was the boy's voice from above. Grabber

shot him a glare.

"This isn't a negotiation, boy. I hold all the dice."

"You mean 'cards', stupid," said the impertinent girl.

"SHUT UP!" Grabber's temper flared, and he savagely slapped the girl on the side of her head. He was losing his composure. It was time to leave. "Let's go, and not another word out of you, whelp."

"You'll pay for that," said the boy, in a voice far too mature and menacing for someone of his age.

"No, I won't. Do not follow me." With that, Grabber pulled Elanir backwards through the kitchen and into the night.

Unalo held a lamp into the cramped cell and inspected the castle's unexpected guest. Then he closed and re-locked the door, shaking his head.

"I will be the first to admit that my knowledge of things agricultural barely rates 'layperson', however..." he shot a withering look at his goblin thief. "I'm fairly confident in saying that is not a scythe, magical or otherwise. In fact, I think there is a very good chance that this room contains a peasant girl, does it not?"

Grabber scowled, but said nothing.

"What happened?"

"The scythe happened. It made me stumble and it struck a post. The ringing woke her up. I'd swear it was yelling for help."

Unalo was about to dismiss this as a pathetic excuse, but paused. The truth was the goblin had been an effective agent for his predecessor, and had shown great skill and competency under Unalo's service as well. If the scythe truly was an artifact of prophecy, which looked increasingly probable, then who knew what powers it contained? He sensed they were on the right path, now he needed to see it through to conclusion.

"The others saw you too, the father and son?"

Grabber nodded. "Yeah, the old man almost got a crossbow on me. And the boy had his hand on the scythe before I even saw him move. That's why I took the hostage."

That was unfortunate. A clever man could link Grabber back to this castle, and its current occupant. Still, the situation wasn't a total loss; the Deepspades were more likely to assume Grabber had been sent by the goblin king in the Vinterlong.

"You've put me in a difficult position. I'll have to hire intermediaries to handle the exchange; that will come out of your retainer. Plus you'll have to lay low for a while, and you won't be sent back to the provinces for at least a year."

The goblin's spine stiffened as though he was about to object, but it never came. Instead, he slumped and said simply, "I understand."

Unalo was about to reiterate his disappointment, but stopped short. It was obvious the goblin's failure offended his sense of professional pride. Anything Unalo said would be redundant and cruel. Not that he objected to cruelty on principle, but cruelty without purpose was… wasteful.

"Good. Now then, I must speak with Holeck about securing the intermediaries."

The note was delivered via longbow. The arrow thumped into the front door just as Ansel closed it from within. Whoever had held the string was a dead-eye shot with a sense of drama.

Ansel tried fruitlessly to pull the arrow out of the door, but it was sunk much too deep. *Strong too,* Ansel thought. He hoped never to be under this man's eye. He untied the note and brought it inside where his father sat at the table.

"What does it say?" Yorick asked.

Ansel unraveled the parchment and held it taut. The script was blocky and crude, doubtless to throw off any handwriting samples. Ansel had no trouble reading it;

despite being farmers, his father had insisted that all of his children would be literate.

"It says we're to come to the third marker east from the Dawson on this road, tomorrow at midnight. We're to bring the scythe to exchange…" Ansel looked up from the note. "Why the scythe? Why not gold, or silver?"

"Because someone thinks it's worth more than either of them, and I'm starting to suspect they're right. Does it say anything else?"

"Yeah, we're to come alone and unarmed, or they'll kill her on sight."

"Hmm, midnight. That doesn't give us much time."

"What do you mean? It isn't until tomorrow night, and it's only a dozen markers down the road. We can be there in a few hours."

Yorick smirked. "We have some arrangements to make before then. I just wish we had enough time to talk to the goblin king, I'd like some answers out of him."

"He wasn't involved," Ansel said firmly.

"You sound mighty confident in that, Son."

"I am. The king was the only one in his village who could speak our tongue, and even then it was broken. But you heard the kidnapper, he was fluent. And the accent, I think he came from one of the cities."

Yorick leaned back to rub his chin. "All right, I'll accept that for now. Get your sandals on, there's someone we have to see."

From his nest on the hill, Pyrce could see the exchange point in its entirety. His associates were already waiting in the shadows of the tree line with their hostage. None of them knew the story behind the assignment, they seldom did, but this job was a strange one. They were hired to exchange a girl of no blood for a simple scythe. At least that was how it was meant to look. In reality, the exchange was staged; it was only intended to draw the targets close.

Even for someone who had built a career out of being the cutout, the whole situation seemed preposterous. While they were being paid very well, a hundred gold crowns a man, the money made the situation stranger still. If there was a reasonable explanation why such large sums were being thrown around for a peasant and a farm implement, it didn't jump out at Pyrce.

Still, they'd been paid half upfront, and the coins were real enough. The forest had offered him the perfect vantage point. Looking down on the exchange point, he had clear sight lines. A road torch illuminated the marker, which would make his targets easy to sight on, while ruining their own night vision. The odds of anyone picking him out of the dark forest were very remote indeed. The doomed farmers wouldn't even know where the fatal shots had come from. Their client wanted no loose ends.

Content with the position, Pyrce wrapped his leg around the bottom limb of his bow and carefully strung it. The string creaked as it took on the full tension of the bow. Then he pulled half a dozen arrows out of their case and planted their heads into the dirt. He'd selected black-painted broad-heads. Farmers weren't likely to sport armor other than leather, which the broad-heads would deal with nicely, and his associates wore scalemail shirts, making any accidents unlikely to cause injury.

In short, this would probably be the easiest hundred crowns he made all year.

The forest was quiet. The birds weren't awake yet, and the autumn chill quieted all but the most persistently sex-starved tree frogs. The hushed voices of his associates floated up to his position. Judging by the cadence and the chuckles, someone shared a rather bawdy limerick.

"Cut the lip-slapping. We're expecting company soon,"

Pyrce called down in just above a whisper. These two were a variable Pyrce didn't care for. While they had come highly recommended, he'd never worked with them before. So far, they were a little more lackadaisical than he cared for.

A rustling came from behind. In one fluid, practiced motion, Pyrce grabbed, knocked, and drew an arrow while he spun around on a heel to face the disturbance. His own night vision had suffered from the marker torch, and it was a moment before his eyes adjusted to the dark. Once they had, he realized he was staring down an arrow shaft at a mule.

The creature noticed him, but regarded him with a dismissive glance before bending down to eat some wild strawberries. Pyrce scanned the area for any other intruders, but saw none. The animal wore no bridal, and its fur was matted with dirt. If it had ever been domestic, those days hadn't been recent. He let the tension out of his drawing arm and returned to his vigil of the exchange point.

Far off in the distance, at the very edge of what his eyes could see in this light, Pyrce spied two figures walking down the road. One carried something long and clumsy in his arms, throwing off his gate.

"Our guests are coming, get ready," he whispered down. They obeyed, and walked out into the light of the torch with their 'hostage'.

The pair stopped as soon as they saw his associates and their hostage step into the road. After a brief conversation, they resumed, but more cautiously. So far, they were following the instructions he'd left on their door to the letter. It was right at midnight, they were alone, and the scythe aside, were unarmed by all appearances.

Good, he thought, *I like it when everyone plays their assigned parts*. Still, Pyrce kept a close eye and a ready hand on the string of his bow. He'd been in the game long enough to see 'safe' situations go bad in the space between heartbeats.

Out of the corner of his eye, he watched the mule walk leisurely into his field of fire. That was a problem. He considered downing the beast for a moment, but dismissed it as too risky. Even with a perfectly placed shot that killed the creature instantly, the sound of a mule rolling down the hill would attract unwanted attention.

Instead, he broke eye contact with their guests and walked over to shoo the mule away. It clopped away indignantly, clearing the sight line once more. The farmers were very close now, and had stopped at the edge of the circle of light cast down by the marker torch. He set his feet in preparation for the strike.

Infuriatingly, Pyrce heard the mule circling back around behind him. He could feel its footsteps as it bungled its way through the forest. The infernal creature was close enough that he could smell its musk. He tried to shut it out of his mind and concentrate on the scene unfolding below. He heard a metallic *clank* behind him, like a horseshoe hitting a rock, but why would a wild mule be shod?

Curious, Pyrce turned around to investigate. To his horror, a calloused hand shot out of the darkness and clamped down on his throat like a bear trap. Another hand appeared and drew Pyrce's own dagger from the sheath at his waist and made two quick, powerful strikes to his chest; one to a lung, one to his heart.

He tried to scream as the hand released, but all the air rushed out of the new exit in his lung. As blood streamed out of his chest, Pyrce fell to the dirt. Before the darkness stole the last of his vision, he looked up at his killer. An enormous, bare chested man returned his gaze. His eyes drifted downward, and the last thing Pyrce saw was too many furry legs, and hooves where one would expect feet.

Huh, a centaur, he thought serenely. *He used the mule for ambush, clever devil…*

Ansel looked over at his father nervously, hoping to find some comfort or strength in his face, but it was stone. Elanir was there, hooded and bound. He gripped the handle of his scythe for reassurance. It helped, but not as it had in the forest.

Yorick was the first to break the tense silence. "So, how do you want to handle this?"

The larger one to the right stepped forward and spoke. "First, the boy'll set the scythe on the ground by his feet, slowly."

His father gave Ansel a slight nod. He did as instructed.

"Good. Now, just stand there for a second…" The thug gave a little wave towards the hill, and then looked back at them, smiling with anticipation. Heartbeats rolled past, but nothing happened. His smile faded.

"Oy, Pyrce," he shouted towards the hill. "You picked a poor time for a piss."

The sharp *twang* of a bowstring sounded from the woods, and an arm-span long arrow planted itself into the dirt of the road barely a hand away from the thug's feet.

"Hey! Careful, numb-fingers. That almost hit me!"

The bow twanged again, and the arrow atoned for the inaccuracy of its predecessor by auguring straight through the thug's neck, erupting out the back with a spray of crimson. The man collapsed to the ground, gurgling blood and clutching his ruined throat.

"Ansel, now," Yorick said with supernatural calm. On his command, Ansel did as they had rehearsed and snatched up the scythe. No sooner than it was back in his hand, Ansel felt a surge of feral energy. He honed in on the surviving thug and charged ahead with deadly focus. Yorick ran for the fallen man's weapon and plucked it from the dirt.

The straggler's first impulse was to draw his own sword, but he couldn't bring it up in time for a block, Ansel was too fast. Propelled forward on a plume of incoherent rage, he drew the scythe high into the air above him, then used every last inch of its reach and savagely brought it down on the brigand's outstretched arm. The blade didn't even pause as it sang effortlessly through skin, tendon, and bone.

The ruffian screamed with anguish and shock as he pulled back his stump of a left arm, but Ansel hadn't finished. He slid to a stop, then raised his weapon again, the man's exposed neck firmly in his mind.

"That's enough," his father said, but Ansel wasn't listening. The scythe tugged gently at his hands, eager for the strike. His muscles tensed and began the swing that would decapitate the man who dared to harm his sister.

It froze in midair. Ansel looked up to see an iron fist gripping the scythe's handle.

"I said enough. We need him alive, for the moment."

The implied threat hung in the air as Ansel continued to loom over the injured man. Yorick walked over to where the hooded Elanir lay and gently nudged her with a foot.

He sighted heavily. Using the bastard sword he'd recovered from the perforated man, he slashed open her belly. Ansel looked on in confused horror as straw intestines spilled onto the road.

"A dummy!" Ansel said. He looked back to the man he'd maimed. "You double-crossing bastards, where is she?"

"Patience, Son. I expected this." Yorick cut the belt from the fallen man's scabbard. He used it as a tourniquet on the survivor's stump. The man's face was pale, his eyes distant and unfocused. Yorick gave him a hard slap to the face to return him to the here-and-now.

"Do I have your attention? Good. Now, listen carefully: ambushes can be confusing, so let me explain your situation." Yorick crossed his arms over his barrel chest. "You are the only survivor. We guessed about your archer on the hill and sent someone to neutralize him. It was our man that fired the arrows, so you have no back-up. This one…" He gave the dead man a contemptuous little kick. "Is quite dead as well."

"As for you, well, my son has effectively, ahem, disarmed

you. And on my word, he'll be only too happy to finish the swing for your neck he started. So, if you want *any* chance of getting on with your life, you should start talking. Now."

"I don't believe it." Ansel sat in his usual chair in the kitchen, cleaning dried blood from the blade of his scythe. "The duke has been nothing but polite."

"Beware smiling snakes," Caballus said, poking his head through the kitchen window. The low ceiling inside the farmhouse meant the centaur had to stay outside. If it bothered him, it didn't show.

"But why are you both so sure?"

"Simple elimination, Son." Yorick started ticking points off on his fingers. "First, the men were hired by a man who sounds suspiciously like the duke's right-hand, Horick?"

"Holeck," Caballus corrected. "He's been in that castle for decades. Served the last two lords, in fact."

"Right. Second, they were paid a large amount of gold crowns upfront, with more to be delivered later. Nobody within a two-day ride has that kind of money but the duke, except maybe one or two merchants in town, and even then, that much money would be a huge chunk of their total worth. And third, he asked some pointed questions about your plow the last time we saw him, and he knows you converted it."

Ansel had to admit, the circumstantial evidence was compelling.

Caballus leaned in to rest a forearm on the window sill. "So, where does that leave us? Storming the castle?"

"I'm afraid so. Gerkolis has my little girl, and he's already sent people to kill us. We can't just turn over the scythe, or whatever the hell it is. And even if we could, I've seen the effect it has over you. I don't want him having it. The problem is going to be raising troops."

"Okay, that does it!" Ansel slammed a fist down on the table. He pointed a finger. "You're no farmer, Father. And you!" The finger of accusation turned to Caballus. "You're not a simple plow-hand with a convenient beast-of-burden for an ass. Come clean, both of you."

The two men shared a resigned glance at each other. Caballus merely shrugged. "He's already figured it out, Yorick. No point bailing water once the ship's sunk."

His father's head dipped. "You're right, of course. Ansel, look at me, boy. I am a farmer now, and a pretty good one. But the truth is somewhat more complicated than that. Before any of you children were born, before I met your blessed mother, I was a soldier. A general, actually, and a pretty good one."

"There's that famous modesty." Caballus snorted. "Your old man was the best commander the echelon ever had. Until me, of course."

Yorick rolled his eyes. "Of course. I fought through two of the orc campaigns, along with elves, a tribe of dwarves, and even a lone centaur who never talked about where he came from, and still doesn't."

Ansel sat in rapt attention. "What happened then?"

"I tired of the life, the bloodshed, the endless marches, the constant thirst and near starvation. I got old, Son. When the second orc campaign ended, I met your mother. Your oldest brother grew in her womb only months later. I didn't want the life anymore, and certainly not for her or our children. So, I buried it. Or at least thought I had."

Ansel sat and absorbed this like a thirsty plant. After several long moments of contemplation, he spoke again. "I'm guessing we aren't really 'Deepspades', then?"

"Of course we are, don't ever doubt it. It was the name your mother and I chose for our new life together. You and your brothers and sister came from *that* life."

Ansel nodded solemnly, then turned to Caballus. "What

about you?"

"Same story, just delayed a few years, and no children of course."

"I suppose not, hard to find a wife when you're the only centaur."

"Not as hard as you might think. My wife is human."

"You're married?" Ansel was shocked. The obvious question ran out of his mouth before his brain could corral it. "But then, how do you two…" A mischievous grin spread across Caballus's mouth. "Nevermind! Forget I asked."

With some effort, his mind returned to the problem at hand. "So, we need troops, is that all?"

"Is that all?" Yorick repeated. "We don't just need troops; we need a lot of them, preferably with some fighting experience and their own weapons. Many of the farmers in the province are retired soldiers just like Caballus and I, but many of them are older than us, and many of the rest won't be eager to fight again."

"You know them, Father. Go find the ones who will, and meet me back here in three days."

Yorick couldn't help but smirk as his son started giving orders. "Oh, really? And what will you be doing?"

"It's time I go talk to the goblin king," Ansel said.

"Why? You told me he wasn't involved."

"He wasn't," Ansel said confidently. "But he's about to be."

"It's been four days. They've failed, they must have." Unalo's pace quickened, while heading down the hall towards the archives. The older Holeck strained to keep pace on creaking legs.

"We won't know for certain until they report in."

Unalo shot the man an incredulous look. "Do you really think they're in a position to report anything? They're buzzard feed by now."

"These men were professionals, and came highly recommended. The idea that all three of them were killed by a couple of peasants seems… implausible."

Unalo stopped dead and stared at his chief of staff. "You still don't understand what we're after here, do you?" Holeck opened his mouth to object, but Unalo pressed on. "A weapon of prophecy, ancient and powerful. The dragons didn't commit just any old ramblings to paper. There's no telling how much magic went into its creation, or from whom. The fact your pros haven't returned just confirms its strength, as far as I'm concerned."

If even a peasant becomes as formidable as that boy, just imagine what someone with real strength and cunning could accomplish. Unalo left that thought unsaid, but it hung in the air regardless.

He had already sunk nearly a thousand gold crowns into securing the artifact, he wouldn't stop now. Regrettably, there would be no way to keep it quiet now. Stealth and subversion hadn't worked. He'd have to come at the Deepspades directly.

"Holeck, I'll need you to drum up some charges against the Deepspade family. Treason, whatever. Something heavy enough to justify the death penalty and the confiscation of their farm."

The older man stroked his smooth chin before offering a solution. "Why not tie both problems together? We'll say the hired men had been deputized and were trying to bind the Deepspades for interviews when they were killed trying to execute their duties. That would certainly be worthy of death."

"That could work nicely. We'll need to send someone to recover the bodies. But what if they're identified?"

Holeck gave his master a wounded look. "I didn't hire them for their fame in the province. Quite the opposite, in fact."

Unalo put up his hands. "All right, no offense intended. Draft up the charges and distribute them to the guards. I want to see posters in the square of each village and at every crossroads by week's end."

"Understood, Sire. What, if I may ask, about the girl?"

"Ugh, don't remind me. She's still useful as leverage in case they hatch any fool-hearty plans for revenge. She stays here for now as a hostage."

The Deepspade daughter held in the castle's bowels had proven to be nearly as much trouble as her brother and father. They had to bind the girl's hands after she'd gone for Unalo's ceremonial dagger. Then they had to gag her on account of the incessant screaming, taunts, and a rather vicious bite she'd inflicted on one of his guard's forearms. She had spirit, he couldn't deny, although it did beg the question why anyone would willingly take her back without being paid to do so, and handsomely.

Love was a peculiar type of magic in its own right. In a

father's eye, it could turn a rabid dog into a princess. In a young man's eye, a homely barmaid became a queen. Unalo had sworn off it at an early age.

The Vinterlong forest fell silent as Ansel passed through. Whether it was to show deference, or in anticipation of him falling into another snare trap, he couldn't say. Stump, fortunately, had elected not to run off in the middle of the night on this trip.

The blood trail that had led him to the goblin city was long gone. They'd gotten lost the first night, and Ansel burned an extra day stumbling around the vast woods trying to regain his bearings. Eventually, the scythe grew impatient and started tugging against the straps lashing it to the saddle. Before he'd left the farm, Ansel had converted it once more, this time into a war-scythe. Now the blade was mounted straight up on a new, unbent handle. The handle itself had two grips wrapped with leather to prevent slipping.

Ansel grabbed the scythe's shaft and gave it a firm shake. "Oh no. I ended up hanging by my feet the last time I took directions from you." But the scythe was persistent, and continued to tug in his hand.

"Fine, whatever." He unlashed the handle and held it out in one outstretched hand. It eagerly swung to the west. "Well, I suppose it would have to be a pretty big snare to catch a whole mule, eh Stump?"

His mount's ears turned back, signaling some reservations with his master's logic. They followed the scythe's direction and found the familiar fallen oak by the light streaming through the hole in the canopy.

Ansel's feet dropped to the forest floor with a crunch of pine needles and fall leaves. He walked towards the upturned tangle of roots that camouflaged the entrance to the goblin city, then thought better of the scythe and planted it in the ground before continuing.

He stopped a respectful distance from the portal and drew himself to his full height. "I am Ansel Deepspade, and I wish to talk to the king."

Nothing happened for a long time. Ansel was tempted to repeat himself, but stood resolutely instead. The goblins knew he was there. Their eyes had probably been on him since the moment he crossed the tree line.

Finally, the twisted and spiraled roots parted, disgorging the immensely tall (for a goblin) king of the goblin's subterranean city. His large eyes blinked uncomfortably in the sunlight.

"You brave, Ansel, to return alone, and no seeds."

Ansel bowed slightly. "I have news of the seeds, and hope for your people. The seeds to save your crops are stored in the castle to the north east."

"Why there and not here with you?"

"Because the duke, my *king*, wouldn't release it. He wants the goblins to trade something of equal value for the seeds."

This did not sit well with the king. "Trade what? We starve! Have no things left. Wait longer, I trade bodies of my brood, is that 'equal value?'"

"I understand, and I tried to explain, but he wouldn't listen."

"So why you here? Come to tell me we start raids again or die?"

Ansel shook his head. "No, there is another way. A way we can help each other. The duke holds something precious to you, he also holds something precious to me."

"Go on."

"My sister, my broodmate, was kidnapped a week ago, by a goblin."

The king bristled. "Not one of mine. I order no raid on you."

Ansel put up his hands defensively. "I know, I know.

I'm not accusing you. We believe this goblin was working for the duke. He wasn't like you or your people. He was... different."

"Different?" His eyes narrowed to slits. "Talk like humans? Dress like you? Step through shadows?"

Ansel nodded. "Yes, exactly."

The king sneered. With so many tiny teeth, it was an unsettling sight. "I know his name." He almost spat out the statement.

It took a moment for the full weight of the king's words to settle. Then he remembered; goblins didn't share their names freely. To know a goblin's name was to know them very, very well.

"He's part of your village?"

"No." He shook his head slowly. "Part of my brood. Brother. Dangerous, him exile long time."

"I see." Ansel decided to bring the conversation back on point. "Well, he kidnapped my sister, and then two men tried to kill my father and I. They worked for the duke, and we think that Elanir is in the duke's dungeon. We *know* your seed is there."

"What you want from me, then? How we help each other?"

Ansel took a deep breath. He knew what he was about to propose was unprecedented. All the other races had formed temporary alliances during times of need; elves, dwarves, humans, even orcs once long ago, had all fought together against common foes. But not goblins. They had been the perpetual boogie-men throughout recorded history. They had never worked with anyone but themselves. Then again, they had never established villages or agriculture, either. Maybe this one truly was different. Ansel hoped to learn his name someday.

He took the plunge. "My father is combing the whole province right now, recruiting volunteers. We will march on the castle and either convince him to turn over my sister, or take her by force. Join us, and you will have the seed to save your village."

The sun fell towards the horizon on the third day when Ansel crested the hill to the only home he'd ever known. The wind carried unsettled voices up from the farmhouse. The closer he came, the louder they grew.

Ansel tied Stump off to his post and made his way to the front door, war-scythe in hand. Caballus's rump stood just outside the kitchen window, his tail swatting away at a particularly determined horsefly. A heated exchange flew inside between at least a half-dozen different voices.

Ansel was about to knock when his hand stopped short. Why should he knock? This was his house, after all. With a dramatic flair, he threw the front door open, then entered slowly, blade first. The argument died down immediately.

Crammed throughout the house were over a dozen people. Ansel recognized several of them from the party his father had organized for the rescue in the forest. He knew a couple others from town, but the rest were complete strangers. Ansel realized every eye in the place was turned to him and his now-famous weapon.

Yorick, sitting at the head of the table, cleared his throat. "Gentlemen, this is my son, Ansel." He spread his arms to encompass the entire houseful of guests. "Ansel, this is our army."

"Very good. This will be plenty," Ansel said, far more calmly than he felt.

Someone snorted loudly. "Oh, you think so, child?" It was one of the men Ansel didn't recognize. "Because I was told we were storming a castle. We need heavy weapons to take down the guards, but they're too big to sneak in. We'll be hacked to kindling."

Ansel set down the scythe and crossed his arms. "We won't have to sneak in. We're going right through the front gate."

This was met with nervous laughter from several of the recruits. "A bold plan, to be sure. But there's just one small problem. If they see us coming up the road in full battle dress, they'll *close* and *lock* the gate. That's the whole point of gates."

Ansel shot the man a cold glare. It was just convincing enough for the laughter to cease. "I have the gate under control. It will be open by the time we reach it."

"How do you conjure to do that?"

"I have resources."

"Like what?"

Ansel knew full well the man wouldn't believe him if he told him, so he deflected the question. "It's important they stay secret for now."

The heckler threw up his hands in exasperation. "You're a farm hand! What resources could you have, mule manure? Because it's getting pretty deep in here!"

Yorick slapped a palm down on the table, just hard enough to grab the man's attention. "That's enough, Flint."

"Oh, come now, General, you're not buying into this?"

"As a matter of fact, I am."

Another man spoke up, but with more respect in his quiet voice. "I'm sure I speak for all of us, General, when I say we trust your integrity. But you must admit that the judgment of even the most hardened of us can become… murky when our children are concerned."

"Yeah, exactly my point," Flint resumed. "What say you, Caballus? Do you support this mad boy's plan?"

The centaur smiled dismissively. "Why not? I underestimated him once, and he made a fool of me for my trouble. I wouldn't mind watching him make a fool of you, too."

This time, the snickering had a different target.

"Good, it's settled then." Ansel picked up his scythe and struck the butt on the floorboards. "We're leaving now. We'll reach the castle tomorrow night. The attack begins just before dawn."

It was cold on top of the wall. Fall was in full swing and the wind relentlessly chipped away at the guard's body heat. He'd spent the entire night at his post, keeping non-existent hoards of orcs and invaders from the frozen north at bay. His arm had grown tired slaying so many imaginary enemies with his short sword. Now, the promise of sleep tugged relentlessly at his eyelids.

There was less than an eighth of a candle left before his replacement was due to arrive. With any luck, he'd be in his bed before the sun rose. The torches ringing the castle wall had dimmed through the night as they burned up their fuel. Here and there, one had already winked out. The overlapping shadows played coyly throughout the courtyard.

The guard's drooping eyes could be forgiven, then, for missing the three tiny figures taking advantage of the gaps in the light to silently scale the wall on the far side of the keep. His sleep-deprived mind could be excused for dismissing them as tricks of the light as two of them hunched down and rounded the wall towards the gate. One might even pardon his ears for mistaking their alien-sounding footsteps for a bear passing through the woods. But no one would absolve him for standing there, slack-jawed, as the gate slowly opened, seemingly of its own volition.

It took his mind several precious seconds to catch up with what his eyes were seeing. He'd stood watch over the gate almost every night since being hired by the new duke back in the spring. It had been the most uneventful, boring six months of his entire life. Now, something big and important was happening, and he didn't know what to do.

Sound the alarm, stupid! he chastised himself. His feet engaged, and he ran to the guard shack where the bells were housed. Once they started ringing, over two dozen heavily-armed men would come pouring out of the castle in less than two shakes. He reached the shack and pulled the pins out of the hammer that kept bumbling guards from sounding false alarms.

His hand on the rope, his muscles tensed as he was about to yank down to set the bells in motion. But just as the slack went out of the rope, he felt a burning pain erupt in his right side, stabbing deeply into his core. He craned his neck around to see what had happened, only to feel the pain ratchet up another unbearable level as something sharp and hard twisted inside his kidney.

In the flickering light, he made out giant eyes and dozens of tiny, pointed teeth. His emaciated attacker was no larger than a child, but its face possessed none of a youth's cherub-like innocence, only a stinging malice.

The surge of fear and combat hit him like a falling boulder. Without thinking, he grabbed the unholy creature by its misshapen face and smashed its head into the closest bell. The great brass cone rang out its warning into the waning night. His attacker bounced off the bell like a child's ball, but shook off the impact and lunged for his throat.

The guard tried to deflect the creature, but his arms weren't fast enough. Double rows of tiny teeth sunk into the soft flesh around his windpipe and blood-ways. Curiously, it didn't hurt. Maybe it was the shock of it all. The guard fell backwards from the impact and landed heavily just outside the shack. He could taste coppery blood seeping through his ravaged neck and into his throat and started to cough. The world faded quickly, but streaming out of the castle came the rest of the guard, armed and ready to face the threat. He'd done his job after all. With a small smirk of triumph, the guard let himself drift off to sleep.

"They didn't get him in time." Yorick turned up to face Ansel mounted on Caballus's armored back. "The guard's coming out to meet us."

"Gods dammit!" Ansel leaned forward to get a better look. "The gate's open. We go now!" Ansel dug his heels into Caballus's flanks and thrust his war-scythe into the air. "CHARGE!"

Miraculously, the motley assembly followed without question. Unencumbered by a harness and plow, Caballus exploded towards the gate like a bolt from a crossbow. Ansel's free hand held fast to the twin falchion scabbards crossing the centaur's back. The initial shock of his speed passed, replaced by a thrill welling up in Ansel's throat.

"Yah!" He raked the horseman's sides, eager for more speed.

Caballus glanced back in irritation. "You don't actually have to spur me, you know."

Ansel had enough sense to look just a little sheepish. "Sorry."

The horseman looked forward once more and set his lance hard against his side. Ansel did not envy the poor soul who met its tip at this speed. Even still, as they barreled down the roadway towards the gate, their foes organized into ranks. They were well-equipped, alert, and efficient.

In a fair fight, they would likely wipe out Ansel's force without sweating up their armor. Fortunately, Yorick the General knew something of war; a fair fight is always the result of poor planning.

A single burning arrow arched through the sky over Caballus and Ansel's heads. At the signal, the shadows to either side of the gate came alive. Dozens of goblins, few taller than a single arm-span, poured in through the gate, careful to leave a path for the charging centaur and the rest of the troops. They moved to the flanks of the guard formation, hurling sling stones and short, poisoned spears.

To their credit, the column of guards adjusted quickly, moving into a defensive, three-sided box to counter the sudden appearance of the goblins. But Caballus had reached a full gallop, his horseshoes pounding the earth beneath like meteors. He tucked his lance up under an armpit and set his sights on the guard at the left corner of the formation. Corners were always a weak point; each man exposed two sides to the enemy instead of only one.

The scythe vibrated relentlessly in Ansel's hands, pulsating more so with each step. For a moment, he could have sworn he heard the singing of angels. He raised the blade towards the heavens, twisting his torso to the side in preparation for a single, massive downward swing.

A shock-wave of transfered energy jolted Ansel through his seat as Caballus's lance pierced straight through his target, as well as the man behind him. The crack of thunder sounded as the lance snapped midway down its length, sending a cloud of splinters in every direction.

The change in momentum started Ansel's swing prematurely, but the scythe seemed to guide itself towards a target. It dug deeply into a guard's unprotected neck, cutting through chainmail and down to his sternum.

Caballus dropped the handle of his ruined lance and drew the twin falchions from their scabbards. Ansel had to pull back hard to release the scythe from the grip of the dead man's ribcage, then choked up on his grip for easier close-in fighting.

He'd never fought from a mount before, never had any training of any kind, yet the motions came easily as the guards adjusted again to the breach in their ranks. The singing blade *wanted* to fight; all he had to do was follow its lead.

The rest of his ragtag army caught up before he and

Caballus became completely surrounded. The fighting broke down into man-on-man battles, small mutual-defense groups, and waves of crazed goblins breaking against the castle defenders. Wherever they went, Caballus and Ansel were at the heart of the battle. Combined, they were by far the biggest threat on the field, and the guards knew it.

They threw desperate blows against the centaur's armored legs, trying to bring him down. Every time Ansel would connect with his scythe blade, hands would grab at the shaft and he'd have to fight to recover it. Finally, a lucky strike from a haphazardly thrown hand-ax struck Ansel in the temple. The wedge failed to connect, but the impact still sent stars streaking through his vision.

Ansel tumbled from his perch atop the centaur and hit the ground like a sack of bricks.

"My Lord, you must wake." Even half asleep, Unalo recognized the urgency in Holeck's strained voice. He fought to climb back into full consciousness. As his vision adjusted to candlelight, he could see that his chief of staff's face was every bit as tense as his voice. Unalo's alarm grew.

"What is it, Holeck?"

"The castle is under attack, Sire. The report was sketchy, but it sounds like a mixed force of mercenaries and goblins."

"Goblins? Fighting alongside men? That's impossible."

"The messenger was quite certain, 'Milord."

"Rouse the guard and send them to the wall with crossbows."

Holeck shook his head. "It's too late for that; the attackers are already inside the wall. It appears someone opened the gate for them. We have to move you to a safe place, 'Milord."

"Forget it." Unalo threw off his silk sheets and stormed to his cabinet. "Which merc' group is it? The Jackals?"

"Unknown, Sire, but they are definitely irregulars. Well equipped, but not uniform military."

"At least it's not an invasion force, then. They're testing us."

"Who, Sire?"

"If we're lucky, a neighboring province instead of one of the cities." Unalo threw on a padded undershirt in preparation for the deeply embossed breastplate shining back at him from the cabinet. "They're probing to see how we react. If they were confident of our weakness, they would have just sent their regular troops. But that means we must win today, or a stronger attack will come before we can recover."

Unalo had expected something like this since his ascension, although the presence of the goblins was troubling. He slipped into the breastplate and cinched it tight. Then he pulled a slim rapier from its place in the cabinet and strapped it to his belt. There wasn't time to don any more intricate armor or weapons, but if he was right about the scroll he'd found in the archives last week, armor would hardly matter.

Caballus felt immediately that his rider had been thrown clear. While his falchions swept and arched through the night air, he positioned himself over the boy, his four legs set around Ansel like a protective cage.

"Yorick!" he bellowed. "Ansel's down!"

The former general's head snapped up, as though someone had landed an uppercut to his jaw. He charged at a dead run, cutting through the undefended back of a guard unlucky enough to stand between a father and his son.

Yorick reached the circle of castle defenders trying in vain to take Caballus down. The centaur had accumulated many superficial slashes, scrapes, and gashes, but none of them appeared to slow him down in the least. So focused were the guards on trying to subdue the monster, they overlooked Yorick entirely.

With a vicious swing of his broadsword, Yorick took a man through both kneecaps, just above his greaves. The newly 'short' man collapsed backwards while what remained of his legs kicked frantically. Yorick reached beneath his centaur comrade and grabbed his stunned boy by the collar. Amid the ringing of swords and the screams of the wounded, he jerked him back from the bulk of the castle guards still on their feet.

Ansel was dimly aware of the ground dragging along underneath him. It stopped, and he felt a sharp crack against his cheek, then another. He heard someone shouting urgently, but distantly, as if from the far end of a tunnel. Crawling towards the sounds in his mind, the world started to return.

"Ansel, get up. You have to move."

It was his father's voice. Ansel opened his eyes onto the chaos of battle. Shrugging off the fog in his throbbing head, he staggered to his feet. A score of guards and peasant troops lay dead, alongside the crumpled bodies of a heart-wrenching number of his goblin allies. Caballus was still on his feet… hooves, but his coat of fur was slick with sweat and stained with patches of dark blood. Yet he fought on. What would it take to actually bring him down?

A glint of metal caught Ansel's eye; his scythe lay on the ground not twenty arm spans from where he stood. His hands felt empty and longed for the comfort and power of the blade. His feet started to tread towards the weapon of their own accord, but his progress was halted by a massive forearm around his chest.

"No. You stay out of it," Yorick warned.

Ansel pointed to the spot behind Caballus where the blade lay. "The scythe, I need to get it."

But his father wasn't listening. Yorick stared intently at

a spot on the second floor of the castle. Ansel followed his gaze up to a balcony where a man stood defiantly above the throng. Even in the dim torchlight, Ansel knew it was Gerkolis. The duke wore a brilliantly polished breastplate and a thin sword at his side, but little else.

In the duke's outstretched hands, he held a scroll. He read from it loudly, and as he did so, gossamer tendrils of emerald light began to snake and twist from the parchment. Ansel had never seen anything like it.

Yorick, on the other hand, did not suffer from his son's inexperience. "Spell scroll! Everyone DOWN!"

Ansel wasn't sure what that meant, but it sounded bad. There wasn't much time. "Caballus, my scythe!" He pointed to it.

The centaur looked back to Ansel, then down to the blade lying in the dirt and gore of the battle. With one powerful kick of his hind leg, Caballus sent the scythe spinning wildly through the air like a falling maple seed. Ansel ducked under his father's arm and dashed to intercept.

He lunged over the body of a fallen peasant, then skidded to a halt and threw his hand into the path of the whistling blade. At the exact moment his fingers closed around the shaft, the duke finished reading. Ansel's head turned back towards the fight just in time to see the gossamer strands creeping from the scroll flash a brilliant light.

Everything stopped.

Unalo stepped onto the balcony to survey the courtyard. He was greeted with a scene of carnage. The report was true; dozens of goblins lay slain among the bodies of the irregulars and his guards. But the tiny creatures were the least of his concerns. For a moment, he thought he saw the attacking commander fighting from horseback among a circle of castle guards, until he realized that man and horse were one creature.

Caballus, he thought. This wasn't a mercenary group sent to test him, it was a peasant uprising, and where the centaur was... His eyes scanned the surviving attackers. It didn't take long to find the boy. A merciless smile touched Unalo's lips when he spotted Yorick Deepspade dragging the motionless body of his son away from the throng of guards fighting to take down the centaur.

He couldn't tell if Ansel was dead or merely unconscious. More importantly, however, his hands were empty. Unalo searched the ground desperately for the artifact. He overlooked it on the first pass because it had changed again, but spotted it on the second. The 'scythe' had been re-positioned in line on a new, straight shaft. An awful arrangement for harvesting crops, but probably very effective at harvesting men.

A murder of crows flew overhead, eager for the battle to conclude so they could feast. At last, his goal was within his grasp. Unalo pulled out the scroll and, trying to ignore any misgivings he had about its identification, began to read the enchantment. Tendrils of magical energy coalesced and started clawing through the air.

Below, someone shouted a warning; he'd been spotted. Worse, the boy was back on his feet and headed for the scythe. Nearing panic, Unalo rushed the rest of the incantation. The world flashed and the threads of magic dispersed to the breeze. The scene was utterly silent. Then something struck Unalo on the shoulder with a thump. He looked to the floor and saw a crow frozen in midflight. It was joined a moment later by another, then another.

It worked. Excited by his success, Unalo surveyed the courtyard. Everyone, peasants, goblins, and guards alike, were frozen in place like marble statues. Several fighters caught off balance at the moment the spell fired toppled over.

Actually, it had worked too well. He'd somehow expected

the spell to be smart enough only to freeze the attackers, but no matter. Unsure of how long the effect would last, he hurried through the hallway and down a spiral staircase to the courtyard where he would collect his prize.

Ansel stood frozen within his own body. He strained to move, but not even the smallest facial muscle would obey his commands. Utterly helpless, even his eyes were fixed in place on the balcony. A very content-looking duke tossed the expended scroll aside and disappeared back into the castle.

In the eerie silence, the only sounds were far off birds preparing for the coming dawn, and the steady, inevitable approach of footsteps as the duke made his way through the castle. Immobilized and completely vulnerable, each sound of foot on stone became evermore maddening. The scythe gently vibrated in his hand.

In his peripheral vison, Ansel saw Gerkolis emerge from the main entrance. He strode purposefully in a straight line towards where Ansel stood petrified. But something caught the duke's eye and altered his course. Making his way through the bizarre garden of twisted forms, he stopped in front of its centerpiece; Caballus.

"No point risking you waking up in time to save the day." Gerkolis drew the sword from the scabbard hanging at his side. Its blade was delicate, no thicker than a thumb, but it came to a point as sharp as a pin. Carefully, deliberately moving a scale of armor out of the way, he settled the tip of the blade over the centaur's heart. Mindful to turn the blade flat, thus slipping through the ribs, Gerkolis surged the blade forward with one practiced thrust. The silvered tip erupted out of Caballus's back.

With a sharp tug, he withdrew the blade. "That should do the trick."

Inside his head, Ansel screamed in vengeful rage. His mouth remained fixed, yet the scythe vibrated faster, as if responding to his anger.

The duke's attentions returned to Ansel. With an infuriating swagger, Gerkolis sauntered up to Ansel's side, lethal blade still in hand.

"Hello again, young Deepspade." He produced a kerchief from a trouser pocket and casually wiped Caballus's heart blood from his sword. The scythe's vibrations started to warm Ansel's palm. "I have to thank you, actually. You see, I was about to have you and your father arrested on fallacious charges of treason. Then executed, of course. But I must admit I felt the slightest trace of sympathy for you."

His smile grew wickedly. "But now, you've come here and actually *committed* treason. Imagine my relief! I don't ever need to burden my conscious to achieve my goal." Covetously, his eyes fell onto the scythe. Its vibrations grew so intense that it shook up Ansel's arm bones and through his shoulder. It reached into his ears; he could actually hear it shaking.

Duke Gerkolis spread his feet into a swordsman stance. Like before, he took careful aim over Ansel's heart and placed the tip against the cotton of his tunic. "Do not fear, my good lad, your father and sister will follow you presently."

The heat in Ansel's palm grew to a painful burn. Inside his head, the steady tone of the scythe's vibrations changed. Much to Ansel's shock, in a voice of heavenly splendor, the sword sang a single, powerful word inside his head.

Move!

His outstretched arm fell, and Ansel realized he was once again in control of his body. He pivoted his chest to the side, barely dodging the duke's thrust. The blade sliced cleanly through his tunic, tracing a thin line of crimson across exposed skin.

Overcome with aggression, Ansel brought the shaft of his weapon down brutally on the duke's wrist. It connected, and made a very satisfying wet pop, like snapping a twig wrapped in uncooked bacon.

Gerkolis shouted out in shocked pain and dropped his sword. But before Ansel could adjust his grip and sling his blade around for the duke's neck, his foe had already snatched up his weapon with his off-hand.

Battle-steel struck battle-steel, sending a cascade of sparks into the crisp, predawn air. The two opponents retreated a pace to recover their balance. Scores of statues watched them square off in preparation for the final duel of the day's battle.

Unable to contain his wrath, Ansel made the first move. His scythe sang through the air on course for the duke's neck, but Gerkolis ducked the blow and spun inside of Ansels reach. The vicious tip of his rapier came shooting for Ansel's belly like a serpent's tongue, but the boy dropped the shaft quickly enough to deflect the strike. Instead of his liver, the rapier sunk knuckle-deep into his calf.

It was Ansel's turn to cry in pain. Gerkolis pulled the sword out of his leg and set for a follow-up strike to the chest, but his aim was diminished with the sword in his off hand. The strike went wide of the mark and into Ansel's left bicep.

Reacting purely on instinct, Ansel lashed out with the shaft of his scythe, wielding it like a staff. But Gerkolis had the speed and grace of a trained assassin. In one fluid movement, he blunted the blow with his forearms, then hooked the shaft with the pommel of his rapier, and finished with a swift boot to Ansel's stomach. The kick knocked the wind from Ansel's lungs and sent him tumbling to the ground.

Gerkolis cradled the scythe's handle in the crook of his limped arm. He discarded his rapier with a stab into the dirt then hoisted his prize in triumph.

"Ha! The nerve, the nerve it must have taken to march right up to a castle with a mere rabble and a handful of savages. You really thought you'd win, didn't you?"

Ansel merely growled. But it was a hollow sound. His

courage and anger faded fast without the influence of the scythe racing through his veins.

"No defiant last words prepared?" His eyes focused on the magnificent blade just as the first rays of morning light struck its edge. The effect was mesmerizing.

"Then again, maybe I shouldn't judge too harshly. Holding this, I begin to understand why you believed anything was possible. But your story is that of myth; the peasant boy who finds a magic sword and defeats a tyrant. It's all very stirring, but there's a reason you hear it in bedtime stories and not from the lips of minstrels. Your kind of story doesn't actually happen."

Ansel looked over to the frozen figure of his father, and to his centaur friend. Caballus was already dead, but Yorick would be watching the whole scene in muted horror. Then, powerless to prevent the murder of his son, he would be unceremoniously executed by this monster. He couldn't let that happen. He had to find a way to survive.

Gerkolis switched his grip to overhand then pointed the scythe at Ansel's heart like a spear. "Goodbye, brave boy."

The duke surged forward, intent on driving the tip straight through his foe and into the ground. With a jerky, panicked spasm, Ansel twisted and rolled out of the path of the blade with less than a hand-width to spare. The honed scythe sank deeply into the cool earth. As Gerkolis struggled to free it, Ansel returned to his feet. Seeing an opportunity, he jumped high then drove the heel of his good leg down with all the strength he could muster right onto the scythe's shaft.

The force of the impact snapped the handle like dry firewood, less than a foot behind the blade. Still straining to free it from the ground, Gerkolis was thrown backwards. He kept his footing, but barely.

Running on pure adrenaline and hate, Ansel grabbed the remnant of his scythe's handle and pried the blade loose of the earth's grip with one mighty yank. Carrying the momentum forward, he plunged at the duke, shimmering blade held high in the air like a sword of legends.

Gerkolis saw the attack coming. The rest of the handle's length was still in his hand, and he raised the thick pole to intercept the coming blow. It reached position in time to block the arch of the blade.

Wood met steel.

On any other battlefield with any other sword, the oak rod would have handily halted the attack, and the fight would have continued until either skill or exhaustion won out. But today, on this battlefield, this sword passed through its former handle as if it were no thicker than the stalks of wheat it had cut earlier that season. After all, it was very, very sharp.

Nor did it stop there. It continued to fall, through the polished steel of Gerkolis's breastplate, through his clavicle bone, through a scapula, half a dozen ribs, a lung, and only came to rest after it had bifurcated the duke's cold, shriveled heart.

Ansel spared his fallen adversary no time or words. He jerked the sword free of the steaming wound it had created and limped to his father's still petrified body.

"I know you can hear me. Don't worry; the stabs look worse than they feel. I don't know how to fix you. I hope it just sort of wears off. In the meantime, wait here while I go find Elanir."

He started towards the castle, but stopped and turned back around. "Oh, and I don't know if you saw it, but the duke stabbed Caballus while he was frozen, stabbed him through the heart. I don't think there's anything we can do for him."

Once again, Ansel turned for the entrance, and once again he thought better of it. He looked around for whomever appeared to be the senior most surviving guard. Finding one with a more elaborate helmet than the others, he stood before the man where he wouldn't be missed.

"Hello. Your duke is dead, and from the looks of it, we still outnumber you about two-to-one. So there's no point in more killing and dying on the orders of a dead man. When you thaw out, just lay down your weapons and have a seat."

Finally, Ansel made his way into the castle. He had been here once before, and retained a general sense of the layout. Elanir would almost certainly be kept in a basement level; somehow, Ansel didn't envision her rating a princess's solitary tower just yet.

It didn't take long to find the foreboding spiral staircase leading to the castle's bowels. It was utterly black. Returning briefly to the foyer, he grabbed a torch for light. A musky smell of mold and lingering human misery wafted past Ansel's face as he ran down the stone steps.

"Look, he's limping." Grabber peered through a slit in the former duke's throne room overlooking the main foyer. "He'll have to set the sword down when he reaches his sister's cell. I could finish him easily."

"Unalo thought the same thing." Holeck leaned back in the recently vacated throne. "Observe how well that ended for *him*."

"But it's right there! I'll have a massive advantage in the dark of the dungeon."

"And then what? The scroll won't last forever, and then we'd have to face the rabble outside alone. Even if we did win, which of us would rule? Sword of prophecy or not, do you really think the province would follow an old man or a goblin? No, the spotlight is not our way."

Grabber deflated. "What would you have me do instead?"

Holeck ran his palms over the smooth, warm chestnut of the throne's armrests, and sighed. "What we always do, old friend; wait patiently for the next master to 'serve.' We never need to wait very long. But for now, you should make yourself scarce."

The dungeon floor was slick with condensation, and from the smell of things, less mentionable substances as well. Andel held the torch closer to his nose to mask the stench.

There were only four cells, so the search would be brief. The first was empty, as was the second, but in the far corner of the third, there sat a crumpled pile of dirty clothes roughly the size and shape of his sister.

"Itty!" Ansel pulled on the door. Unsurprisingly, it was locked. "Stay right there, I'm going to find the key." It occurred to Ansel a moment later what a silly thing he'd just said. Where was she going to go? His search for the key was short. A ring of blocky iron keys hung from a nail pounded into the mortar between two blocks on the opposite wall, cruelly within sight, but hopelessly out of reach of those locked away.

He grabbed them and started shoving keys into the lock. Naturally, it was the last one on the ring. The rusted grate door swung inward with an earsplitting creak. He rushed in and propped up Elanir's limp body.

"Itty, c'mon Itty. Be okay, please."

Her face was dirty and streaked with dried tears. She looked exhausted.

"Itty, can you hear me?"

Elanir stirred, her eyelids squinted against the torchlight.

"Ansel?"

"Yes, sweetie, it's me. Father's outside, and the duke can't hurt you anymore. You're safe now."

"Ansel?"

"What is it, Itty?"

"Don't call me Itty."

Ansel laughed then drew her head to his shoulder. "Okay. I won't."

Epilogue

By the time Ansel and Elanir emerged from the castle, morning had arrived in full swing. As he'd hoped, the spell scroll petrifying everyone in the courtyard wore off. The stronger men and more tenacious goblins were the first to thaw.

Yorick was already standing by Caballus's side as his children approached. The centaur was still petrified, probably due to the numerous cuts, bruises, and lacerations he'd already suffered sapping his strength to resist. But as the group watched in silent respect, blood started streaming from behind his scale mail shirt.

To his surprise, Ansel realized that his father was crying. The mighty centaur slowly came back to life, only to collapse to the ground, a look of agonized frustration on his face. Eventually, he found the courage to speak.

"Pressure," he blurted, gasping for air, "put pressure on it."

Yorick rushed in to put a hand on his comrade's chest wound. "Ansel, the other side." Ansel obeyed, and stuck his palm right into the hot, sticky stream of blood pouring from the tiny hole in Caballus's back.

"I'm sorry, my friend," Yorick said, "but there's not much time. He ran you through the heart."

"I know." He struggled to breath. "Good thing that was just the spare. I keep the bigger one in my *other* chest."

"You have two hearts?" Ansel asked incredulously.

"Yes, but don't go spreading it around."

After a few minutes of tending, the bloodflow slowed to a trickle. Caballus stood up on his four feet, while color returned to his face. The spell had faded enough that most everyone stood thawed by then. Surrounded by victorious, celebrating peasants, the castle guards looked to have little fight left in them. They were given temporary quarters in the dungeon.

Someone had the good sense to requisition a keg of ale from the kitchen's stores and the beer flowed freely among the peasants. The goblins declined to drink, but several had to be gently reminded not to eat the bodies of their vanquished foes.

The goblin king found Ansel after himself imbibing more ale than was strictly prudent. He slapped Ansel on the shoulder.

"We find seeds, but human need to come read which bin."

"No problem," Ansel said, swaying gently. "I'll be along shortly to help."

"You all right, for a pink-skin. Big thing you do today, for all of us."

"It was my pleasure to help your people, Great King."

The goblin regarded him for several long moments. "It is, isn't it?" He placed a clawed hand over his heart. "Ansel Deepspade, my name is Durgorath. You are welcome to find me anytime."

A stunned look fell over Ansel's face. "You honor me, Durgorath."

The goblin king shook his head. "No, you honor your people. Good friends, our tribes will be." With that, Durgorath nodded and headed back towards the back of the castle where his prize lay waiting to be identified.

"So this morning…" Caballus said through labored breathing, "You've managed to vanquish an evil tyrant, rescue your little sister, and make peace with one of man's most implacable enemies. Quite impressive, for a plow hand. What will you do this afternoon?"

"Sleep," Ansel replied flatly.

"Ha! And a well-earned nap it will be. I told Flint not to underestimate you. Where is he? I want to rub it in his face a little."

Ansel's mood turned solemn. "It'll have to wait a while. Mister Flint was one of the first casualties."

"Ah." Caballus nodded at the sword still clenched in Ansel's hand. "Your scythe made it through alright, I see. Somewhat shortened, but none the worse for wear."

"Yeah, although it can hardly be called a scythe anymore, more like a sword. Funny, I'd swear it feels happier this way."

"You know, in days past, men gave weapons that helped them achieve amazing feats their own names. Some believed these weapons developed their own souls in time. I'd say a sword like yours has earned a name, wouldn't you agree?"

Ansel peered deeply into the flawless shine of the blade. Its surface reflected his image perfectly, perhaps even more perfectly that a mirror could. Looking into it, Ansel believed he could see himself for who he had been, who he was, and who he would still become, all at once. Somewhere deep in his mind, he felt it singing out to him, a melody of pure tones and emotion. He knew its name.

"Yes, I would." He held the sword up, bathing the blade in sunlight. "I'll call you, *Songsinger*."

Glossary

Aboe- (a-bow) Kingdom on the southern-most peninsula of Terrigan. The kingdom has little or no army, but does not fear being conquered due to the great mountain reaches that surround its borders. Kingdom is wealthy and home of merchants and pirate alike. Of all the kingdoms in Terrigan, it is the most racial diverse with humans, dwarves, and elves, holding political offices.

Aclia - (uh-clee-uh) Black skinned dark angel. She is the most warrior like.

Adoria- (a-door-ee-ah) Kingdom just west of Beykla. It waged a bloody civil war against its western half, Andoria.

Alexis Alexandria Overmoon- (a-lex-us / al-ecks-zan-dree-uh / Over-moon) Daughter heir of King Christopher Calamon Overmoon. High Lord of the Minok Vale. She travels with Apollisian Bargoe, the paladin of Justice, trying to learn the ways of justice to aid her when she becomes queen.

Amerix Alistair Stormhammer- (am-er-icks / ali-stair / storm ham-er) Dwarven general of Clan Stoneheart, formerly of Clan Stormhammer. His clan was wiped out before him, when he was a young man, by dark dwarves and a white dragon. He fled with a few survivors and was welcomed into clan Stoneheart where he excelled in the art of war.

Amyrillion- (amur-ill-yun) Arch-devil of pain.

Androdius- (an-drode-ee-us) Evil black dragon of immense power that lives in the swamp west of Aquabar.

Angelique- (anj-ul-eek) Grayshalk wife of Petrovisk

Apollisian Bargoe- (a-paul-issi-in / bar-go) Paladin of justice that was sent from his order in Westvon keep to oversee the negotiations between the humans and the dwarves from Clan Stoneheart, in attempt to derail a conflict, when he was caught in the middle of the war.

Andoria- (an-door-ee-ah) Formally western Adoria, this kingdom's brief history came when it declared its independence from Adoria. It waged an eight month long war with Adoria, but was eventually re-conquered.

Androdius- (an-droe-dee-us) The great black dragon imprisoned in the swamp west of Aquabar.

Aquabar- (awk-wuh-bar) Capitol of Aten. Lies near the great swamp and the Mountains of Meara.

Arluda- (are-loo-duh) Blue Mistress and friend of Delania.

Artamanake- (art-man-uh-key) Dark dwarven general.

Aten- (a-ten) Queendom to the far west that is ran solely by women. Males of any race are considered inferior and are immediately made into slaves, or killed at birth. Only a choice few males are kept alive for reproduction purposes only. The women of Aten are adept sorceress and keep a rigid society of back stabbing and political maneuvering.

Artez Undermoon- (are-tez) Captain of the Undermoon Darayal Legion

Athodrin- (uh-thod-drin) Souless beings that are created by gods. Demons and angels are some of these.

Ayden- (a-den) Powerful salomen that used Therrig to gain control of a large clan of dark dwarves.

Barbetin- (bar-bet-in) Also known as the Lake of the Damned. It is the lake in the Abyss where damned souls are thrown into the be tortured for eternity by the demons that swim among it.

Beovi- (bee-o-vi) Subterranean fish that live in the deepest freshwater caverns of the underworld. They are a delicacy to dwarves, dark dwarves, dark elves and other subterranean races. These fish can grow to unlimited size, depending on the lake or river in which they live.

Berylys-Quieness- (berry-liss / kwee-uh-ness) Great

White dragon. She disappeared and is rumored to be dead.

Beykla- (bay-kla) Human kingdom on the northeastern corner of Terrigan. The kingdom is well to do, militantly powerful, and well patrolled. It has never, in its long history, been conquered.

Blue Dragon Inn- Inn in Central City that is closets to the Dawson river and the Dawson river bridge, where Lance, Kaisha, Ryshander, and Apollisian battled the dwarven horde, until the king arrived with re-enforcements.

Borkin- (bore-kin) Small wooden device that is inserted into the mouth that keeps the wearer from closing their jaws.

Bureland- (bur-land) small hamlet, in the southern part of Beykla, where Lance spent most of his childhood and early adult life with his adoptive father, Davohn.

Breedikai- (bree-da-kii) Original gods, or gods that were created. They have no soul and most dwell in Merioulus.

Broyed- (broid) Male incubus dark angel.

Bykalicus- (Bye-kal-eh-kus) Powerful arch-demon that controls much of the Abyss.

Cadacka- (ka-doc-uh) Black ceremonial robe worn by elves when they have lost a love one and are mourning. Most elves never remove the cloak once it is donned.

Calours- (ka-loo-ers) Non-sedimentary rocks found in the underworld. Subterranean races, mostly species of dwarves, use them to heat to cook meat on.

Calito, battle of- (kuh-lee-toe) Battle that took place in Adoria near the town of Dolzan. Adorian knights fought against an evil necromancer named Randolph Forelinger who commanded over a thousand undead soldiers.

Carcarass- (kar-kar-us) Training school that raises and trains Aten born pureblood males to be slaves as they age.

Casen- (kay-sin) Name applied to animals that grow to giant size. Named after the halfling wizard Nermal Casen that accidentally created them.

Cathena- (Ka-theen-uh) Falconeer, daughter of Petrovisk.

Central City- City just south of the Dawson Stronghold that is in the center of the Beyklan nation.

Cheural- (Share-uhl) Gadgeteer, daughter of Petrovisk.

Christopher Calamon Overmoon- (Kris-toe-fur / Kal-a-mon / O-ver-moon) High king of the Minok Vale.

Clan Cutstone- Clan that makes its home under the Lalin Plateau in Southern Beykla.

Colonel Mortan Ganover- First lieutenant of Duke Dolin Blackhawk, and acting mayor when the Duke is gone. Is considered responsible for the slaughter at central City by the dwarves due to his inability to act on the paladin Apollisian's recommendations.

Commander Fehzban Algor Stoneheart- (fez-ben / al-gore) Commander and loyal follower of General Amerix Stormhammer. Was tried and convicted of treason after the Torrent manor and the Central City campaigns.

Copel Nin- (cope-ul) Fat keeper of the gladiator slaves in the arena in Central City. Copel was once a gladiator champion but in the fight he earned his freedom he was severely injured, ending his career as a fighter. He was hired by the duke to be the keeper of the slaves. Copel always worked hard at the job but as he aged, his injury and time took its toll on him preventing his ability to stay in shape. He soon became fat, but he enjoyed his job at the arena as he longed for the days to hear the roar of the crowd once more.

Council of Wise- Consists of ten elders that sit on the governing seat at Monk Vale, though not all ten are usually present at meeting, There has to be at least six to hold a vote.

Cranetium- (krane-tee-um) Official title given to an elven high mage. The title means little to other elves, save for the wizards and sorcerers of their Vales.

Crowalta- (Crow-all-tah) Mother of the Black Sept in control of the Gearian.

Dadramedion- (day-drom-uh-dee-in) Powerful arch demon and enemy to Bykalicus.

Dargruden- (Dar-grew-din) Male leader of the Gearian.

Dall-kal-Mour- (doll-kal-moo-ur) Title given to blood born men from Aten. They are the only males that are allowed to reproduce. They are expensive slaves and only the highest ranking, or wealthy own them. It is a status symbol for Mother's, or heads of septs, to own more than one, since they will never give birth.

Dolzan- (dol-zahn) Small city in the north western side of Adoria.

Darayal Legion- (dar-ray-all) One hundred of the finest elite elven rangers that patrol the Minok Vale in pairs. They are skilled swordsman that wield a weapon in each hand during battle. They are as feared as they are awed.

Darious Theobold- (dare-ee-us / They-bold) Eleven year old son of king Theobold.

Dark Dwarves- Dwarves that live solely in the underworld. They have pupil-less eyes that have adapted over time to see in the dark by detecting heat patterns. They hate bright light as it is painful for them, and have turned to wicked and evil ways as a society.

Dargruden- (dar-grude-in) Dal-kal-mour that runs the Gearian.

Darren Brightson, Duke- (Dare-in / bright-sun) Duke of the Adorian lands just to the east of the northeastern border of Aten. Governs over the small hamlet of Lostom.

Darrion-Quieness- (dare-ee-on / kwee-eh-ness) Great wyrm white dragon. Oldest of all white dragons and most powerful. His lair is in the mountains of Nalir, but he roams all over the realms. He often leads lesser races against their enemies, and takes the majority of the treasure after the victory. His last major campaign was in aide of the dark dwarves against the dwarven Clan Stormhammer.

Davohn Ecnal- (da-von) Adoptive father of Lance. He is a woodcutter that made his home in Bureland and found

Lance when Lance was only six years old. He raised him as his son until Lance left when he was seventeen.

Dawson River- Largest river that runs in Terrigan. It stretches from the Sea of Balfour, north of Beykla, all the way through the southern kingdom of Aboe.

Delania- (duh-lane-ee-uh) Beautiful succubus that dwells in the Abyss.

Delker- (Dell-kur) Wizard bent on creating an alliance between powerful allies across terrigan that are interested in defeating established kingdoms.

Demphinshile- (Dim-fin-shy-ul) Dark elf city deep in the under mountain.

Dicermadon- (die-sir-ma-don) God of gods, Dicermadon plots with demons to kill the son of a goddess, drawing the wrath of the gods that he governs.

Diltz Quest- (Dilts) Ceremony in which Dal-kal-mours, Aten full blooded males, compete in a gladiator style competition to be selected as a mate for the queen.

Dolgo seeds- (dole-go) A tasty mountain nut found on the steepest slopes of the highest mountain. Considered a delicacy by all dwarves and mountain people.

Dome of the Rock- Ancient dwarven temple that was supposedly built by Durion himself. The dwarven Mountain God. The temple is rumored to be atop the Lalin Plateau.

Donathuku- (Don-uh-thue-koo) Arch-devil of terror.

Donjurik- (Don-szhur-ick) Small thin greyshalk sword. Rarely used in combat. Primarily ceremonial.

Donk- Aten word for the penis. It is an insulting word in their culture and is associated with weakness and stupidity.

Doogan Raymer- (doo-gun / ray-muhr) Northern noble from Dawson. Doogan is a conniving tactician who has made his estates through double dealing and backstabbing. He shows his family tree as being distantly related to the king, and hopes to one day return his house the throne.

Dorcastig- (door-cast-ig) Tall muscled priest of Rha-Cordan. Follows under Resin Darkhand. One of the priests that participated in the DeNaucght.

Durion- (doog-a thee-in) Dwarven Mountain God.

Dregan City- (dree-gan) Home of the Clan Stormhammer before it was wiped out by the dark dwarves and a white dragon.

Drunda- (drun-duh) The god the orcs follow. It is not known if he actually exists, or even if he is male.

Earth Oath- Oath an elf makes that they will give their lives trying to up hold.

Ecnal- (eck-null) surname given to all orphans of Beykla before they were all killed by unknown assassins.

Eckwon- (Eck-qwon) Trinidy's warhorse when he was alive.

Edsil Strongbow- (Ed-zuhl) Darayal captain of the Strongbow Vale.

Ehleeshuh- (Uh-leash-uh) White unicorn.

Elder Bartoke- (bar-toke) Elder of the Minok Vale, member of the Council of the Wise, and Keeper of the Sealed Passing.

Elder Darmond- (dar-mond) Elder of the Minok Vale, member of the Council of the Wise, and Keeper of the Passing.

Elder Humas- (hue-mass) Elder of the Minok Vale, member of the Council of the Wise, and Keeper of the Passing.

Elder Varmintan- (var-mint-ton) Elder of the Minok Vale, member of the Council of Wise, and Keeper of the Passing.

Elecksixs- (uh-lecks-ick) Succubus leader of the dark angels.

City of Eldred- (ale-dread) Small town that brews their own specific ale that is not revered by most other Beyklan towns.

Erik Stromson- (stahm-son) General of the Beyklan Western army and hero of the orc wars.

Eucladower Strongbow- Oldest Elder of the Minok Council of Wise and Keeper of the Passings.

Famen's Tree- (fay-mens) Large tree three miles east of the Dawson River Bridge. The tree was named after Jeddis Famen, a Central City militia leader that held off an orc attack. After the battle he led a group militiamen after the fleeing orcs, and managed to slay one of the orc leaders as they fled. He nailed the orc's head on a spike to the tree as a message to any other orcs. That was the last orc battle against Central City during the orc wars. The people believed the orcs were afraid of him, but in truth they were massing to finish the elves at the Minok Vale.

Fezbhan Algor Stoneheart- (Fez-ban) Commander of the Stoneheart Clan and cleric of Leska.

Fig root- Strongbow root that is dried and soaked in spirits.

Flunt- God of Fire, and one of the four elemental gods.

Funis- (Fu-niss) Strong straight line of waxed bowstring that was at the draw of all the Proudarrow Bows from the Darayal Legion. This device allowed them to shoot several arrows at once with deadly precession.

Freedom Festival- Holiday celebrated in Beykla to commemorate the end of the twenty year-long orc wars.

Galla noodles- (ga-la) Thin noodles often prepared with butter.

Garlibane- (gar-lee-bane) High mage and Elder of the Council of Wise in Minok Vale.

Gearian- (Gear-ee-in) Collection of incorrigible sudas that exist for the sole purpose of raping and killing women in Aten who have been convicted of the most serious crimes. The women are stripped of their power and thrown into the pit for spectators to watch as they are raped repeatedly over many days until they are killed or die.

General Laricin West- (lair-iss-in) Late general for the northern Beyklan Army that was responsible for scattering the orc horde, in the battle that was later referred to as; The

Quigen. General Laricin and his men fought to the last man, keeping the orc horde from wiping out what was left of the elven resistance.

General Thatcher- (Thach-er) Southern general of the Beyklan Army that embraced the southern Beyklan nobles when they announced their independence.

Gorsan- (gore-sahn) Dwarven brew master who is a distant relative to Fehzban. Gorsan lives in Dolzan and sells dwarven ales to the locals.

Greyshalk- Tall furry humanoids that have strong beliefs in family, tribe, and warfare.

Gregory Herwain- (her-wane) Southern noble that is chairmen of affairs in southern Beykla. He is leader of House Herwain that is well known for saying much and doing little. He hosts the monthly meetings of the southern nobles in the city of Motivas at the House of Affairs.

Grimolikin Hill, battle of- (Grim-mole-uh-kin) Battle where greyshalks were forced from their land by the Beyklans during the orc wars. The Beyklans were actually trying to route several tribes of kriel that were helping the orcs.

Gweits- (ga-weets) Tiny insect like demons that dwell on the rocky floor of the Abyss. They feed on flesh, and burrow under skin with their horrific claws and hooks.

Harbor Mountain- Large city state on the Dalgun island of Aboe.

Heart of the rock- A gemstone mounted on a gold ring that is aid to have magical properties that can prevent the wearer from being harmed by dragon's breath.

Hector De Scoran- (heck-tor / day-skore-an) Evil warrior wizard that is the King of Nalir. Believes that Lance was prophesized to destroy his kingdom, and will stop at nothing until the boy is dead.

Henrious- (hen-ree-us) Ex-Diltz quest gladiator and Dal-kal-mour that helps Tonya of the White and the

Freedom Movement.

Hiramem- (her-uh-mem) Old female sorceress that lives in Aten. She often works for Ramasiel in the red tower and has a limited ability at foretelling. She often uses old chicken bones, stones and other small objects that she tosses about on a board with elven skin stretched over it. She is from Beykla originally. She grew up in Sineuvia.

Hourid Thigguard- (hor-id / thig-guard) Master of Arms and father of Mylaneia.

Ian Silverman- (E-uhn) Human knight under Duke Darren Brightstar. Fought in the Battle of Calito. Has two sons, Ian Silverman the Second and Myer Silverman. Both are adventures and Ian does not agree with their lifestyle.

Ickten Norris- (ick-ton) Ranger that works for the Hentridge Farm south of Central City. He is an expert tracker and skilled swordsman. His favored enemies are orcs.

Illilander tree- (ill-lee-land-er) Largest trees in the realms. Over five hundred feet tall.

Iratus- (eye-rat-us) A rare form of a personality that has the ability to gain great strength from anger.

Jon Klement- Arch-mage of Central Beyklan Army.

Jordan Gersian- (jor-dun / ger-see-in) Southern Nobleman that is leading the plot to pull southern Beykla away from the north.

Jude- (Jewd) Mercenary swordsman from Bureland. He sold his sword to fight brigands, polecats and other minor enemies of Bureland. He is also Lance's best friend.

Jurnda Undermoon- (jern-duh) Dark elf legionnaire that fights with two axes. Big brother to Artez.

Kai-Harkia- (kay-hark-ee-uh) Mountain kingdom northwest from Beykla. Its people are dark skinned, dark haired, heavy chested, nomad swordsmen. They seldom form static villages, though some do exist.

Kalen Al-Kalidius- (kay-lin / al-kal-id-ee-us) Grey elf ex-stepson of King Overmoon of the Minok Vale. Kalen has turned to the shadow and hungers for power, hoping to take over the throne of Nalir when Hector dies.

Kalistirsts- (kal-eh-stirsts) Underground mole people with no eyes that live in the underworld.

Kalliman Theobold- (kall-eh-man) King of Beykla.

Kalliman Castle- (kall-eh-man) Castle and home of King Kalliman Theobold.

Kareeg Hut- (kuh-reeg) Nobleman that owned more land than any other noble in all of Beykla. His lands where in the north that extended from just south of the Torrent Manor all that way west to the border of Beykla and all the way east to the Dawson River right up Dawson itself. His brother was a Captain that was stationed at the Torrent manor when it fell and he hates the dwarves more than any other Beyklan.

Katrinal- (Ka-trine-uhl) Greyshalk daughter of Petrovisk.

Katykop- (Kate-ee-cop) Abyssal for mischievous/feline.

Kellacun- (kell-eh-kun) Wererat assassin that worked for the guild in central city before it was destroyed. Now she works for Kalen in attempt to kill Lance.

Kendalerairy Overmoon- (ken-doll-ler-air-ee) Captain of the Overmoon Darayal Legion.

Kerstap- (kur-stap) Mighty curved two handed greyshalk sword.

King Minostak- (min-oh-stack) Greyshalk king.

Kings, Game of- Game similar to Chess.

Kingsford City- Largest city in Terrigan. Capitol of Ladathon.

Kornicus- (corn-uh-cus) Demon imp and servant of Delania.

Kuma- (koo-muh) Blade attached to the end of the Strongbow's bows for melee fighting.

Kriel- (kree-uhl) Smaller thinner greyshalks with darker fur with spots. Hyena like.

Ladathon- (lad-uh-thon) Southern country, south of Tyrine, where mysterious animals live in thick jungle. Kingsford City, the largest city in the world, is its capitol.

Ladathonian Warhorse- (lad-uh-thone-ee-un) A breed of war horse from Ladathon that stands nearly eighteen hands high and weighs nearly three thousand pounds.

Lalin Plateau- (lay-lin) large plateau that is the middle of southern Beykla. It is covered by thick lush forest and is nearly impossible to scale it's thousand foot high sheer rock walls. Stories tell of ancient ruins at the top, but few have climbed to its summit to validate the claims. What makes the plateau so unique is that the Dawson river runs through the inside of it in a great river cave.

Lance Ecnal- Adopted son of Davohn Ecnal. Lance's birth name is Lancalion Levendis Lampara. His natural mother was Panoleen, the goddess of mercy. Lance is prophesized to bring plague and death on the world, though he sees himself as nothing more than an orphan trying to discover his past.

Lancalion Levendis Lampara- (lance-uh-lion / lev-un-dis / lamb-par-uh) Birth name given to Lance Ecnal.

Larunthus- (lar-unth-this) God of the Hunt.

Leska- (les-kuh) The Earth Mother Goddess. She reins over all living things while they are alive, including plants and animals. She is one of the four elemental gods.

Lirlithe- (lear-lith) Short haired mischievous dark angel with curved horns.

Lostom- (lose-tom) Small Hamlet on the border of Aten and Adoria

Lostos- (low-stoes) Name for the underground complex of the Severed Heart Guild of wererats in Central City.

Lukerey- (lou-kear-ee) God of Luck and Mischief.

Lunarian- (lou-nar-ee-in) Enchanted wells that priestly elves, or other good forest creatures, bless by the powers of Leska to rejuvenate and to heal one another.

Lyndall- (lin-doll) Gladiator champion in Central City. A skilled swordsman that had fought over two hundred forty fights.

Markus- (mark-us) Suda in Ramasiel's tower that is secret lover with Reena

Marlana- (mar-lane-uh) Backstabbing Mistress of the Blue Sept that conspired with Ramasiel to overthrow the Mother of the Blue Sept in order for her to control a second vote in the senate.

Marzahna- (marr-zohn-uh) Mother of the Yellow Sept that was banished for wanting to marry. She built a smaller tower on the border of Aten in the hamlet of Lostom.

Mary of the Yellow Robe- Mistress of the banished yellow mother, Marzahna.

Master David Hentridge- (hint-ridge) Leader of small mercenary guild that is disguised as a farm, just south of Central City. King Theobold uses them to hunt and kill orc's that he does not want the public to know exists, keeping their awareness of the actually amount of the green skinned beasts that still live in his kingdom.

Merioulus- (mare-ee-oh-you-lus) City of the Gods. Set on a form of the astral plane.

Mersaat- (mare-sat) Great Blue Dragon that lives in the Desert of Tyrine. A scroll was stolen from his lair by a hapless thief. The scroll was sold several times until it ended up at the great library in Kingsford City where Ladathon scholars identified the text as draconian. What made the scroll unique was that it was written in humanoid size. Few humans know draconic. It gave credibility that there is a secret sept of priests that worship the great serpents, but it led others to believe that the once the beasts fully mature, they gain the ability to transform into a man-like creature. All of these theories are yet to be proven.

Mershaulk- (mur-shalk) God of Serpents. Some believe the god does not exist and is only worshipped by a cult following known as the Sept of Serpents. Mershaulk is also the term referred to for men who go into berserker rage in in battle. The rage is so intense the men do not feel pain, can continue to battle long after their body has died, and have a hard time differing friend from foe on the battle field. Mershaulks are as feared as they are respected as warriors, though they never fight with comrades as a Mershaulk often claims the lives of those around him in his rage.

Midagord Milence Stormhammer-Amerix Stormhammer's deceased father.

Minok Vale- (my-nock) Name of the elven sovereignty that is set in Beykla.

Mordrik- (more-drick) Dark Elf mercenary that resided in the under mountain. Amerix Stormhammer hunted him and killed his band one by one for killing a Kalistirst friend of his.

Mortigalus- (mor-tuh-gal-us) Arch-Devil of Gluttony and Torture.

Motivas- (moe-ta-vis) Southernmost city in Beykla. City is built on a large brick foundation that is rumored to be ruins of an ancient civilization.

Mountain Heart- Home city of Clan Stoneheart, located in the Pyberian Mountains.

Mount Steeple- The largest mountain on Terrigan. The mountain is rumored to hold the road way to Merioulus as its peak cannot be seen as it ascends into a permanent veil of clouds.

Mowaka- (moe-walk-uh) camouflage cloak like blanket that elven archers, and sometimes rangers, use to spy on their enemies.

Myer Silverman- (my-er) Son of Ian Silverman of Lostom.

Mylaneia Thigguard- (my-lane-ya / thig-guard) Young daughter of Hourid Thigguard, and courtier of Tharxton Stoneheart.

Nalir- (nall-er) Evil southern empire that is made up primarily of swamps and quagmires. A militantly powerful nation that worships most of the evil gods.

Necromidus- (neck-rom-eh-dus) A collection of the first four tiers of necromancy spells.

Osimar- (0ssy-mar) City on Dalgun Island that makes the best wine in all of the realms. Most expensive.

Oswald Thorrin- (oz-wald / thor-in) Captain of the Royal Beyklan Guard and bounty hunter, though he only collects on lawful bounties set by the magistrates.

Panoleen- (pan-oh-leen) Goddess of Mercy that was banished from the heavens.

Pav-co- (pahv-coe) Fat wererat guild leader in Central City.

Petrovisk- (pet-roe-visk) Old greyshalk champion from the orc wars.

Plaatu- (pla-two) Kalistirsts friend of Amerix that was killed by one of Mordrik's dark dwarves.

Pyberian Mountains- (pie-beer-ee-an) Mountain range in the northwest corner of Beykla, near Adoria.

Quadry Proudarrow- (quad-ree) Darayal Legionnaire of the Minok Vale.

Quigen- (kwi-jin) Elven word for sacrifice. Most widely known as the name of the great battlefield where General Laricin West scattered the orcish horde by fighting until every man in his army fell in the Serrin Plains.

Ramasiel- (ram-uh-zeal) One of the three mothers of the red order in Aten. She is a powerful sorceress and a political power in Aquabar.

Randolph Forlinger- (ran-doff / four-ling-er) Powerful necromancer that was defeated and slain at the Battle of Calito.

Reagle, The- A fancy clothing store in Aquabar that makes dresses and other articles of women's clothing. It does not make any article of clothing that could be used in an intimate way to make the women more attractive. Atenians believe that men have no right to be attracted to women, that the act should be gratifying to the woman only.

Reena- (ree-nuh) Third sorceress, also called third sister, of the red sept in Aten. Second only to Ramasiel herself.

Rha-Cordan- (rah-kor-don) God of Death and Dying. Not inherently evil, he reigns over the placement of souls when they enter the afterlife, though he has been known to be incredibly vengeful to those who prolong their lives through magical means.

Salomen- (sall-oh-men) Subterranean humanoid species with powerful mind controlling abilities.

Samarkel- (suh-mark-uhl) Large frog-like demon from the Abyss.

Serrin Plains- (sare-in) Dangerous expansive grassland just south of Minok Vale where most of the evil races that live in Beykla dwell.

Sha-Shor'Nai- (sha-shore-nigh) God of the Sun and Light.

Shanorian- (sha-nore-ee-uhn) General of devils.

Sierra Blackhawk- Duke Dolin Blackhawk's granddaughter.

Silas Proudarrow- (sigh-less) Darayal Legionnaire of the Minok Vale.

Stephanis- (stuh-fawn-is) God of Justice.

Stieny Gittledorph- (stie-knee / get-tull-dorf) Halfling thief who became mixed up with the dragon Darrion-Quieness.

Stormghast- The great stone doors that seals Mountain Heart from the dark uncharted reaches of the undermountian.

Suda- (sue-duh) Title given to all non-eunuch slaves in Aten. A suda is looked as a lower form of a man by the Tuda, or eunuch.

Surelda Al-Kalidius- (sir-el-da / al-kuh-lid-ee-us) Ex-wife of King Overmoon and mother of Kalen Al-Kalidius.

Surshy- (sir-she) Goddess of Water. One of the four elemental gods.

Tallnok- (tal-knock) Young wizard that works for the Hentridge Farm south of Central City. Occasionally hires himself out for specific jobs.

Talwin- (tall-win) Young apprentice war wizard that joined the Western Beyklan Army instead of staying with the mage guild in Dawson..

Targavian Hollen Stoneheart- (tar-gave-ee-in / hall-in) New general promoted by Tharxton after the betrayal of Amerix and his officers.

Terrigan- (ter-eh-gun) Name of the continent that all known civilizations exists.

Tharxton Stoneheart- (tharx-ton) Young king of Clan Stoneheart and political rival with Amerix Alistair Stormhammer.

Therrig Alistair Delastan- (ther-ig / al-eh-stair / del-eh-stan) illegitimate son of Amerix Alistair Stormhammer. Therrig is living proof of Amerix's and Therrig's mother's infidelity.

Thomas Smith (Arwar)- (are-wahr) Blacksmith that was worked at the Torrent Manor before Amerix attacked. He was head of the liaison between the two peoples and He learned dwarven from his many dwarven friends at Mountain Heart before he retired and moved back to Poria.

Tonya- Former mother of the white tower, who staged her death so that she could anonymously lead the Freedom Movement of Aten.

Torrent Manor- small keep northwest of Central City that was built specifically for enforcing the trade embargo on the dwarves that dwelled in the Pyberian Mountains, and the Adorians in the civil war.

Tracy Ross- Young girl that lives with her family at the Junction outside of the Torrent Manor.

Trinidy- (trin-eh-dee) Dead paladin of Dicermadon, that was raised from the dead by evil priests of Rha-Cordan creating the first death knight.

Trishal- (trish-uhl) Multi-armed female demon with human torso and snake body.

Tuda- (too-duh) Title given to all eunuch slaves in Aten.

Tylergaiden Proudarrow- (tyler-gai-den) Darayal captain of the Proudarrow Vale

Tyrine- (tie-reen) Kingdom south west of Beykla..

Valley of Mist- Lush green valley that is just below the entrance to Mountain Heart in the Pyberian Mountains.

Vendaigehn- (vin-day-gun) Type of horse from the Plains of Vendaiga. The steeds are marked with white spots n their flanks, and are taller than most horses with longer, thinner legs. Legend says that Vendaigehn steeds are the off spring of a pegasus and a unicorn, though hat has never been proven.

Victor DeVulge- (day-vul-juh) Slain squire of Apollisian Bargoe.

Vinr- (Vin-er) Greyshalk word for friend.

Vlargcar- (va-larg-car) Orc whelp saved by Amerix when he and his mother was ordered killed by their tribe.

Vrescan Alistair Delastan- Therrig's father that was killed fighting side by side with Midagord Stormhammer in defense of Dregan City.

Walter Thigpen- Middle aged royal guard crossbowman and longtime friend of Captain Oswald Thorrin.

Westvon Keep- (west-van) large keep and hamlet to the far east in Beykla on the banks of the Dawson River.

Whisten- (wiss-ton) God of Air, and one of the four elemental gods.

Yahna- (ya-nuh) City in the heavens where mortal souls, blessed by their gods, dwell.

Yohr-Acht- (your-awk-tuh) Great green dragon that makes his lair atop the Lalin Plateau.

About the Author

Patrick S. Tomlinson lives in Milwaukee, Wisconsin with a menagerie of houseplants in varying levels of health, a Mustang, and a Triumph motorcycle bought specifically to embarrass and infuriate Harley riders. When not writing sci-fi and fantasy novels and short stories, Patrick is busy developing his other passion for writing and performing stand-up comedy in the Madison, Milwaukee, and Chicago scenes.

Go to www.Zod001.com and Join for Free!

Other New Babel Titles

Core Series
"The Plea of Apollisian"
"The Trial of Innocence"
"Darrion-Quieness"
"The Death of Kings"
"Tides of Winter"
"Return of the Father"
"The Sword from the Sky"

Core Series Collector's Books
"A Prisoner's Welcome"
"The Breach of Crowns"
"Exodus of the Strong"

Other Novels
"The Wererat's Tale"
"The Wererat's Tale-Of Rat's and Men"
"The Wererat's Tale-Ring of the Nonul"
"The Wererat's Tale-The Collar of Perdition"
"The Wererat's Tale-Tiers of Valdore" 2016

"White Wraith"
"White Wraith-The Journey"
"White Wraith-The Lock of Requ" Summer 2016
"White Wraith-Maelstrom Serpents" 2017

"The Forge of Feasts" Dwarven Cookbook
"Walk the Abyss" Abyss Walker Anthology

"The Apocalypse of Enoch"
"The Apocalypse of Enoch I-Rapture"
"The Apocalypse of Enoch II-Scourge"
"The Apocalypse of Enoch III-Desolation"

The Apocalypse of Enoch World Setting
"Children of Enoch I-Dark Harvest"

Graphic Novels
"Orcs and Generals"
"The Apocalypse of Enoch-Rapture" Kissell Studios 2016
"Vindicated Inc" Kissell Studios

For additional NBB titles, visit: www.newbabelbooks.com

www.ingramcontent.com/pod-product-compliance
Lightning Source LLC
LaVergne TN
LVHW050647100826
845148LV00011B/2027

* 9 7 8 1 6 3 1 9 6 0 2 5 3 *